ALSO BY L

Grant Wolves Series

Early Grave
Shallow Grave
Grave Threat
Grave Legacy
Grave Origins

Standalone Books

Ghost Magnet

Anthologies

Undead Tales
Dark Shadows 2
Before, During, and After

CHAPTER 1

I could hear the patient screaming even before the back doors of the ambulance burst open. That was never a good sign.

"Ricardo Villareal, Hispanic male witch, age thirty-two, altered mental state," the paramedic in the back said while his partner climbed out of the driver's seat and jogged around to the back to help unload the patient.

I helped the EMTs maneuver the gurney out of the back of their rig, listening carefully through the patient's screaming as the paramedic, Andy, continued.

"Patient collapsed at a convenience store. Clerk made the call. No one on site knew what, if anything, he was on. He presented with classic signs of opioid overdose, so we administered naloxone on the scene."

I winced. Naloxone was used to reverse the effects of opioids. If the patient was this agitated from withdrawal, he'd probably need to be sedated before we could do anything for him. Hell, even restrained, he could be trouble if he started throwing magic around. Not many practitioners could sling a proper spell in an altered mental state, but I kept a careful eye on him anyway—not that there was fuck all I could do about it but get out of the line of fire.

"Get them off! Get them off!" Ricardo shrieked, writhing and straining against the restraints that held him in place for his own safety.

I put a gentle hand on his shoulder. "Hi, Mr. Villareal. I'm Emily. Can you take a deep breath for me? You're going to need to calm down before we can remove your restraints."

His eyes locked on me, so wide with panic I could see white all the way around his deep brown irises, "Please, señora, get them off! *Serpientes! Serpientes!*"

Snakes? I glanced at the resident, Dr. Russell Carson, but he was busy checking vitals as we prepared to move the patient into the hospital proper.

"How long has he been like this?" Russell asked.

"The whole way back, pretty much. About ten minutes," Michelle, the other EMT, said. "His stats improved about twenty seconds after Andy gave him the naloxone, and he was stable for maybe thirty seconds after that before he started freaking out. It took both of us to restrain him. Fortunately, we weren't on the road yet."

I gave the patient's shoulder a reassuring pat. "There aren't any snakes, Mr. Villareal. You're at Saint Vincent Hospital. You collapsed. Do you remember what you took?"

He just kept howling about snakes. I made a mental note of the heart rate and blood pressure Russell rattled off to me as we wheeled the gurney into the ER. The EMTs trailed along behind us. They needed their gurney back, and protocol demanded they stay with the patient until an ER doctor or nurse signed the proper form anyway.

"Where are we going?" Russell asked next.

"Curtain four," I said. "Everything's ready."

As soon as the gurney was parked, I grabbed a pre-loaded syringe from the trauma cart and slapped it in Russell's hand before he could finish asking for it. He flashed me his trademark smile, the one that regularly melted the panties off women when he wasn't even trying. I was immune to his charms. I'd seen him with his wife, who was both disgustingly beautiful and a lovely human being to boot. But even if he hadn't been hopelessly devoted to her—which he was—I didn't shit where I ate.

While the doctor administered the sedative, I beckoned Andy over so I could sign the paperwork with a sweep of my finger across the tablet.

"Hey, Michelle and I are going out for drinks after our shift. You interested in coming along?" he asked.

I glanced past him at his wide-eyed partner, who shook her head and made a slashing motion across her throat. Chuckling as I passed the tablet back to Andy, I shook my head. "Sorry, I can't tonight. I've got a date."

It was true, too. Nice to not have to make up an excuse on the fly. I'm a shitty liar.

"What about you, Russ?" Andy asked.

Russell deposited the used syringe in the sharps container. "Can't, sorry. Dinner with the in-laws."

I snickered behind a hand when I spotted Michelle sagging in relief. She'd had a thing for her partner for years, but Andy was oblivious. He was like a big dumb puppy, utterly adorable and enthusiastic about everything but as unobservant as a tree stump when it came to social cues.

"I've got an idea," I said, killing time while we waited for the sedative to take effect. "Why don't you two make a night of it and have dinner and drinks?"

Andy rubbed his clean-shaven jaw, then shrugged. "Might as well, I've got nothing better to do tonight. What about you?" He glanced at Michelle, whose expression turned cool in a hurry. I winced on her behalf. Big. Dumb. Puppy.

"Sure, whatever," she said, giving her dark ponytail a toss.

Right about then, Ricardo went quiet. I glanced his way, expecting to see him snoozing peacefully, but instead found him spasming on the gurney.

"He's seizing!" I rushed over and quickly began unfastening the restraints holding him to the gurney. Russell helped me, but once Ricardo's arms and legs were freed there wasn't anything we could do but stand by, wait for the seizure to run its course, and make sure he didn't fling himself off the gurney.

Habit had made me glance at the clock when I noticed the patient seizing. I shifted my eyes between the patient and the clock while we waited, keeping track of approximately how long the seizure lasted. Just past the ninety-second mark, Ricardo lit up like a Christmas tree. Magical energy radiated from his body from head to toe, pulsing erratically.

I grabbed Russell and shoved him away from the gurney. "Everyone out!"

Russell stumbled a few steps before digging his heels in. "Hey!" He couldn't see the magic. None of them could.

I glanced over my shoulder. The whole gurney was vibrating under a still-spasming Ricardo, despite the fact that he was now levitating a few inches over it. Russell must've looked back too, because he stopped fighting me and hurried forward, spreading his arms to herd Michelle and Andy out too. Once we were clear of the curtain, I grabbed it with all intent to pull it shut. The curtains in the ER were warded with basic protection spells that kept most magic from penetrating them. It was our only line of defense against witches lashing out with magic. Tranquilizer guns would've been preferable, but Public Relations had ix-nayed that suggestion handily.

My eyes caught on Ricardo as I slid the curtain on its track, stopping just short of closing it completely. He'd stopped seizing but still hovered over the gurney, pulsing with golden energy that intensified by the second. The overhead lights flickered as the intense aura of magic radiating from him interrupted the electrical current running through them.

"Emily, close the curtain!" Russell said.

I hesitated a moment more before crossing the threshold and closing the curtain behind me.

"No!" Michelle shouted on the other side, but she didn't part the curtain at my back. No one did.

They were afraid, and rightly so. An out-of-control witch is a danger to everyone around them, but themselves most of all. I ran for the trauma cart and ripped open the top drawer, scattering supplies all over the linoleum floor in my haste to obtain another pre-loaded syringe. Syringe in hand, I hurried to Ricardo's side, uncapping it on the way. The lights flickered again, the air so full of crackling energy that my ponytail started to stand up.

I reached for his arm, but as soon as my fingers touched his skin, he flung them off and sat up. He looked down at me, the whites of his eyes glowing along with the rest of him. A shiver ran down my spine, and my fingers tightened on the syringe. If I couldn't get at his arm, any big muscle would do. I didn't like my chances of getting a needle past his faded blue jeans, however.

"Ricardo, can you hear me? It's Emily. I need you to calm down, buddy."

A sweep of his hand sent a rush of magic in my direction, the spell spinning in the air and solidifying a fraction of a second before it slammed into me. I flew backward, careening into the trauma cart and knocking over the IV stand in the process. My death grip on the syringe was the only thing that kept it in my hand. I leaped to my feet, heart racing, suppressing the urge to hold the syringe aloft in triumph like a ballplayer after a gravity-defying catch.

Voices rose on the other side of the curtain before it parted, and Russell slipped back into the space. The movement drew Ricardo's attention, and while he was distracted, I darted forward again—grateful for the no-squeak soles on my nursing shoes—and jabbed the needle into his shoulder and depressed the plunger. Ricardo howled in outrage, but I quickly ducked out of sight. First rule of magic: You can't cast at what you can't see.

Unfortunately, Ricardo could still see the doctor. I sensed a surge in the magical energy above me, and my heart rose into my throat.

"Duck!"

I watched between the gurney's metal legs as Russell hit the deck, and the curtain behind him ruffled as whatever spell Ricardo had flung dissipated harmlessly on impact. Those damn curtains never ceased to impress me. I wished, not for the first time, I could get a warded set of scrubs. I'd looked into it once, but it proved too expensive since the rigors of regular washing would make the magic wear off quickly, and sometimes I went through two or three sets of scrubs in one shift.

Rather than getting his mundane ass back on the other side of the curtain where it belonged, Russell quickly scrambled closer, taking up a position on the opposite side of the gurney. I glared at him, hands fisting in frustration. But the gurney's legs had ceased to vibrate, suggesting that the second dose of sedative was doing its job.

The magical glow emanating from Ricardo gradually dimmed, and the gurney eventually creaked when his weight settled back onto it. The air lost its magical charge. I counted to thirty before poking my head up. Ricardo lay inert on the thin mattress, eyes closed. The only lingering trace of his power was the kernel of magic tucked away inside him that all witches possessed.

All witches but me, anyway.

CHAPTER 2

My heroics didn't earn me Employee of the Month, but at least I didn't get canned. After a full-bore ass-chewing about flouting protocols and endangering myself and others, my supervisor sent me back to work with a stern warning to keep my nose clean—and the bonus implication that if not for the fact one of my colleagues was on maternity leave, I would've been suspended.

At least she didn't reassign me to psych.

Truth be told, I probably did deserve some sort of disciplinary action for administering a sedative to a patient without being ordered to by a doctor, but Russell covered my ass on that one. I made a mental note to send him a fruit basket, or maybe a tongue depressor bouquet. Whatever one sends to hot doctors as a thank you that couldn't be misinterpreted as anything else.

The ER was slow enough that I managed to stay out of trouble for a few hours by sticking to inventory-related tasks, though I did check in on Ricardo the Ticking Time Bomb on my break to make sure he hadn't gone supernova again. He'd been admitted for observation and was still sleeping off the double dose of midazolam.

"Emily, with me."

I looked up from the drawer full of compression wraps I'd been dutifully counting, completely losing count and blinking as I struggled to reconcile the terse voice with the familiar doctor striding briskly toward a nearby curtain.

Bob was an older gentleman, one of the nicest doctors in the ER—if not the world. The embroidered script on his white lab coat read "Dr. Robert Jenkins, M.D." but everyone called him Dr. Bob. He was great with kids. His brusque tone was, therefore, concerning. I caught a colleague's eye and shot him a questioning look. He just shrugged. I abandoned my task and hurried off after the doctor.

In the ER, you never know what's going to be on the other side of the curtain. The fact that it was a full moon shift made it even dicier. Strange shit happens on the full moon. Grandmothers decide to swallow the family jewels. Teenagers get the bright idea to superglue their genitals together.

Seriously. Strange shit.

This time, all that lay behind the curtain was a gurney with a young woman on it. No blood, no guts, no gore. In fact, there was a complete lack of the hysterics that so often accompany trips to the ER. The woman lay there quietly with her hands at her sides, her chestnut hair a riot of curls in stark contrast to the smooth white pillowcase beneath her head. Her pale green eyes were open, but she didn't react to either Dr. Bob's arrival or my own. She simply lay there, staring blankly at nothing. The lights were on, but no one was home.

There was something familiar about her, but I couldn't

quite put my finger on it. I could swear I'd seen her before, but where?

"Caucasian female without ID, found on a plaza bench in an unresponsive state." Dr. Bob read aloud for my benefit, his normally paternal voice stiff and wooden. At least, until he turned his attention fully to the patient. "Miss? I'm Dr. Jenkins. Do you know where you are?" He leaned over to shine a penlight in her eyes and check her pupillary response.

I went through the motions, grabbing a blood pressure cuff while I tried to figure out where it was I'd seen the patient before. It's not like Santa Fe is a big city, but I lived in my little bubble just like everyone else. The market? My favorite Chinese place? The bank?

The cafe!

It struck me suddenly, and I must have made a noise because Dr. Bob cast a glance in my direction. Clearing my throat, I busied myself with slipping the blood pressure cuff on the unresponsive woman's arm. She didn't even blink. A shiver ran down my spine, even as I reeled from my sudden revelation.

The doctor made a few notes on his tablet, then slipped it into his white coat's big pocket. All business again, he turned to me. "Take her vitals and get her into a gown. Let me know when it's done, and if there's any indication we need to do a pelvic."

His uncharacteristic demeanor finally started to make sense. He was concerned that she might be a rape victim, and if memory served he had a granddaughter about Jane Doe's age. While it was entirely possible, given what I'd realized about our patient, I doubted it.

You see, Jane Doe was a regular at my favorite cafe. The petite, vivacious twenty-something met friends there often, and they'd always stood out to me even though no one else paid them any particular mind. Why? They were practitioners.

I wish I could say I could tell because of their body language, witchy manner of dress, or some other tell. Sherlock Holmes-style deductive reasoning. But I've always been able to tell the difference between witches and mundanes. A curse of my witchy heritage, I suppose. Even though I didn't have a scrap of magic to my prestigious Davenport name—to my mother's eternal embarrassment—I could still sense it around me and see it in others whether I wanted to or not. It's like the universe got a kick out of taunting me. Laughing at me. I tried not to take it personally, but it could be distracting.

But the magic that had once made Jane Doe shine like a beacon to me... There was no trace of it now. Its absence told me all I needed to know about Jane Doe's mysterious condition. She'd burned herself out.

I'd only ever encountered one burned-out witch before, a distant cousin who had overextended himself trying to heal his dying father. Healing magic is powerful, extremely difficult, and very few witches actually have any talent for it. Even those who do can overreach easily enough. His father died despite his best efforts, and for all intents and purposes, my cousin did too. He spent the rest of his life in a wheelchair, attended by a full-time nurse because he couldn't—or wouldn't—even urinate without assistance.

"Now he's just like you, Null!" Dan, my younger brother, had taunted.

It was far from a fair comparison, but try arguing that with a seven-year-old. My cousin had lost his gift. I never had one in the first place. And yet, despite my "disability," I'm a fully functional human being. Burned-out witches are little more than empty husks. Poor Jane would never be the same again.

But I couldn't tell Dr. Bob that. He may have been the world's nicest guy, but no one I worked with knew I was anything but a mundie. I preferred it that way. That didn't mean the itch to put his mind at ease wasn't there.

"Yes, doctor," I said.

I'm not sure he heard me before the curtain swished shut behind him. Sighing, I turned my attention back to the comatose woman on the gurney. The best way to alleviate the doctor's concern was to do what he'd asked me to. As for Jane, she deserved the same care, the same compassion I'd give any patient.

I performed my tasks with due diligence, finding no sign of injury along the way, no irregularities with her vitals, no indication of any kind of assault. Dr. Bob returned to complete his examination and ordered blood tests and imaging. But her blood work and scans would come back clean, because what was wrong with her wasn't something science could fix. She would never be whole again. As someone who had never been "whole" to start with, I couldn't begin to understand what she was going through. But I did wonder how she'd ended up that way.

CHAPTER 3

The rest of my shift was pleasantly uneventful, even for a full moon. My shift ended at six, and by six-forty-five I'd finished changeover, showered and changed, and was on my way to the restaurant to meet my date for the evening. Jane Doe was still in the back of my mind as I drove the short distance from the hospital to the restaurant. I'd wanted to check in on her before I left, but I didn't have time. I'm pretty sure Matt timed it that way on purpose so I wouldn't have a chance to back out.

Matt had been my best friend and self-appointed love guru since we broke things off. I think he felt guilty; I was his last girlfriend before he came out of the closet.

Okay, that's understating it a bit. I was still his girlfriend when he came out of the closet. Now, there are basically two things that can happen in that situation. One, you hate the person and your self-confidence is diminished for the rest of your life. Or, two, you get the hell over it and remain friends. The way I think about it, Matt and I always had a connection. It just took us a while to figure out what it was. I'm not saying it wasn't a shock, or that I didn't need some time to process it. But in the end, I decided that my life was vastly better with Matt in it than it was without.

A few of the dates he'd set me up on since then caused me to question that stance. What did it say about me that the only way I could get a date was for my gay ex to fix me up? I tried not to think too hard about that.

Tonight's selection—jeez, I make him sound like a wine—already had one strike against him: his name was Barry. I know, I know, I shouldn't have been so judgmental. Don't judge a book by its cover, yadda, yadda. In this case, I hadn't even seen the cover, so it was more like judging a book by its title. Anyway. It's just a name. Right?

But have you ever met anyone named "Barry" that didn't belong in 1985? It sounded like someone's weird uncle from an '80s family sitcom. A name to be spoken with playful exasperation. "Oh, Barry!" Men my age weren't named Barry, which was probably why I was eyeing a silver fox at the bar speculatively when the well-groomed stranger approached me.

"Emily? Wow, your picture doesn't do you justice." His voice was deep, melodic, like warm honey.

I looked up into the bluest eyes I'd ever seen, and for a long moment, I was struck dumb. Speechless. Like that ever happens. Ever. Guess there really is a first time for everything.

"Are you okay?" he asked with concern. I must have been staring. I felt my cheeks flush... Oh, good grief, I was actually blushing in front of this bright-eyed Adonis. Definitely a modern vintage.

"Uh, yeah. Yes. Sorry, hi! I'm Emily. I hope you're Barry and not some creepy stalker," I said, making an attempt at humor while admonishing myself inwardly. *Looks aren't everything. Get a grip, Em.*

But looks, he had them. Chiseled jaw, twin dimples flanking a generous smile. Straight, white teeth. Short blond hair, but long enough to run your fingers through or grab a handful of in the heat of passion.

I was so not imagining running my fingers through his hair while he was introducing himself.

"Ha! No. If that were the case, I would have said you looked much better in person than through binoculars," he said, accompanying the quip with a playful wink. Good-looking and a sense of humor, to boot. Best of all? Not even a hint of magic in him.

Laughing, I let him guide me to the hostess stand so we could be seated, and I settled in to get to know Barry better.

"Matt tells me you're a ski instructor at the resort?"

He nodded. "Yup. This is my second winter. I have to admit, when I heard there was a ski resort around here I was skeptical."

Laughter bubbled from my throat. "I can understand that. All the pictures you see of the desert southwest are parched landscapes in warm tones, right?"

"With colorful sunsets in the background," he added, with a chuckle.

"Yeah, I thought it'd be that year-round when I moved out here. I got a rude awakening that first winter. They get quite a bit of powder in the mountains, but even down here we average something like twenty-five inches per year."

"It's good for business, at least. My business, that is."

Smiling, I nodded. "Yeah, I guess it would be."

The meal passed pleasantly enough, with light conversation flowing steadily throughout. When we finished, the waiter discreetly made our plates disappear. It was the sort of place where they'd pack up your leftovers and bring them to the table in a little sack, which I always felt was preferable to having someone drop off a styrofoam container and expecting you to pack it up yourself. Okay, maybe on some level there's still a little bit of spoiled rich kid inside of me.

It wasn't until after the table was clear that the question I'd been dreading came up.

"So, how did you and Matt meet?"

"Drag show," I joked. Matt was so not that kind of queer.

Barry laughed, but in that knowing way that said he was in on the joke. "Aw, come on. Really."

I fidgeted with my napkin and floundered for a response, certain Barry didn't realize we were poised on the precipice of more personal territory. I never know how to answer that question. It was complicated. Embarrassing. You'd think I would've given it more thought, since Matt setting me up on blind dates wasn't an unusual occurrence. Deciding to go the literal route, I folded my napkin and set it on the table in front of me in what ought to be a universal signal for "no dessert, thank you" even if it rarely actually worked.

"It's not a very exciting story, really. We were neighbors when I first moved to town. I think I met him at the mailbox or something. It's not like apartment dwellers exchange casseroles or anything."

"Oh, that's great. I never really thought about it, but now that you mention it, I don't know anyone in my building but my roommate. It's funny how that works. As close as we all live to each other, I can't even say I know anyone's first name." He drummed his fingers thoughtfully on the table.

"Yeah, tell me about it. I work weird hours sometimes, too. Night shifts. They probably think I'm some kind of vampire."

He chuckled. "But vampires don't exist, do they?"

"Not as far as I know."

A flicker of movement in the corner of my eye caught my attention, and I looked over to see our waitress approaching with a single plate and a big smile. Her hand was cupped around the front of a flickering candle to keep the little flame from guttering as she approached the table.

My cheeks heated, and I glanced at Barry to find him smiling from ear to ear, dimples on full display. I snatched my napkin from the table just in time for the waitress to set the plate in front of me.

"Happy birthday," she said, then made herself scarce.

I sat there awkwardly, staring at the tiny chocolate cake in front of me. I could feel the eyes of curious diners on me and shifted uncomfortably in my seat.

Barry leaned forward in his chair, resting an elbow on the table. "I hope it's okay. Matt said you didn't like to make a big deal out of your birthday, so I asked them not to sing. But I hated to let it go completely unremarked."

"It's fine. Thank you." The words sprung to my lips automatically. I could at least pretend to appreciate the gesture. I pursed my lips to blow out the candle.

"Make a wish," Barry said, stopping me short.

I didn't put much stock in wishes, but Jane Doe's face flashed through my mind. I didn't think there was anything to be done for her, but I wished for her soul to find peace before blowing the tiny flame out.

When I looked up, Barry was watching me with a thoughtful expression. I plucked the candle from the cake and set it aside. "What?"

"Just wondering."

I wasn't sure I'd like what he was fishing for, but I bit anyway. "Wondering what?"

"Why you don't like to make a fuss over your birthday. You're too young to be sensitive about your age."

Chuckling, I moved the sugar caddy and shaker set out of the way and slid the plate into the center of the table. He wasn't wrong. I was only twenty-eight. "I wasn't aware there was a minimum age for that. Help me eat this, will you?"

"So, that's it then? You don't like to be reminded about getting older?" He grabbed his still-clean butter knife and sliced the tiny cake in half.

"Eh, not really. My relationship with my birthday is... complicated." To say the least. I took a bite of the cake, which was just as tasty as the rest of the meal had been. Granted, I've never met chocolate I didn't like.

"Complicated how?"

The guy was relentless. I grimaced, taking longer to chew than necessary as I put on my mental tap-dancing shoes. "I'm not sure this is first-date material, but... my birthday was never a cause for celebration. I'm kind of the disappointment of the family."

"I can't begin to understand how that's true. You're beautiful, smart, have a successful medical career..."

I snorted. "Matt told you I'm a nurse, not a neurosurgeon, right?"

He smiled. "Even neurosurgeons need nurses."

"Granted." Point for him. "Let's just say that no matter what I do with my life, it'll never be enough for my mother. I quit trying ages ago."

"Does your family live around here?"

I laughed. "Oh, hell no. I came all the way out here to get away from them. What about you?"

"Colorado. I'm just here for the winter." He paused for a beat, and those dimples came out again. "Well, unless I find a good reason to stick around."

Charming devil.

BARRY PAID FOR DINNER. He also kissed my hand and didn't try to walk me to my car. Chivalrous without being overbearing. Another point for Barry. On the whole, it was a nice date, but I was glad it hadn't lingered too late. It had been a long day, and I wanted to go home, kick off my shoes, and relax before I had to get up and do it all over again the next day—minus the date, that is. It might have been Tuesday, but it was my crazy schedule's version of Thursday, and I was feeling the late-week fatigue already. Being on your feet so much is tiring, no matter how used to it you get.

Snow began to fall while I was driving home, dusting the city in a layer of fresh powder. I could hardly believe it was already December. The year seemed to go by so quickly. Time may fly when you're having fun, but it also tends to fly any other time you're not really paying attention to it. Two more years to the big three-oh. By the time my mother was my age, she'd already had four kids, myself included. Just another way I'd never be like her, I suppose. Granted, not popping out a half-dozen kids was probably the only thing about me she approved of. I doubt she wanted me further muddying the bloodline with my inferior genes.

I pulled into my usual spot in the parking lot. They're not numbered, but it's a small enough building that everyone tends to gravitate toward a particular spot by unspoken social agreement. The scent of wood smoke from countless chimneys lingered in the air, tickling my nostrils when I opened the car door and following me up the stairs to my second-floor apartment. I remember thinking that the building's adobe facade was so charming when I moved in. After a few years, it just looked... brown. There's a lot of brown in Santa Fe.

I could tell the door was unlocked by the lack of resistance to my key turning in the lock. I hadn't bothered changing the locks or asking Matt for his key when he moved out. A single gal sometimes likes to know that there's someone out there who would a) miss her if she fell off the face of the earth and b) find her body before her cat started to eat her. I suspected Matt was holding down the couch, lying in wait for me to return so he could pump me for information.

Though I usually enjoyed his visits, dread suddenly gnawed at my stomach. I loved Matt, but sometimes a girl just needs some downtime at the end of a long day. Granted, coming home to Matt after a long day used to be one of my favorite things. I took a breath and put on a smile before pushing open the door, a quip poised on my tongue.

"Don't you have a place of your own or something?"

"There you are, birthday girl!" He beamed at me from the couch. "I was starting to wonder if Barry had knocked you out and thrown you in the trunk."

Mention of my birthday made me remember I was supposed to be annoyed with him. "You're the one that ought to be worried about head trauma. You told him it was my birthday."

He wrinkled his nose. "He didn't make a fuss, did he? I told him not to make a fuss. I didn't mean to tell him. It just slipped out the other day." He sat up a bit and pointed at the mismatched pair of Christmas-themed mugs on the coffee table. "Hey, did I mention I made cocoa? Come get some."

"Don't try to distract me with gourmet drinking chocolate." I huffed quietly, though I wasn't really upset and he knew it. Matt makes the best cocoa, with real chocolate and everything. Cooking is his superpower. It's one of the things that won me over back when we were dating.

He sat back with a smirk and draped an arm along the back of the sofa. "Well, how did it go?"

"Let me get my shoes off at least." I unwound my scarf and peeled off the rest of my outerwear, hanging it all up on the coat rack inside the door before slipping off my "date shoes" and padding in stockinged feet over to the couch. Yeah, I was stalling, and it wasn't just because Matt was so fun to torment.

He waited mostly patiently, one knee bouncing. "Ok, your shoes are off. Don't leave me in suspense! I mean, you didn't bring him home, so I guess it could have gone better."

I rolled my eyes. "Right, because that has ever happened with a blind date you foisted off on me." He held out a mug to me, and I accepted it with murmured thanks, curling my fingers around it and lifting it to let the fragrant steam tickle my nose. It was nice and warm, and I wondered if a little bird named Barry had reported I was on my way home. That was one of the problems with Matt's blind dates. I never knew where their loyalties lay.

"There's a first time for everything. Now, out with it!" Judging from the tone of his voice, he was one more deferment away from hitting me with a pillow. Out of deference to one of my few actually nice shirts and his culinary prowess, I decided not to push my luck and risk ending up wearing my cocoa. But I did take a small sip of it, savoring its richness and depth of flavor.

"It was... fine," I said eventually, which summed it up.

"Fine? Ugh. You're impossible." He snatched his own cocoa from the coffee table and sat back against the arm of the couch, turned toward me with one leg tucked under him. "He's cute, right? Polite. Witty. And he has a job."

I winced at his emphasis on the job bit. "Never going to live that down, am I?"

"You're the one that dated a hobo."

"He wasn't a hobo! He was just... between places. You know how it is."

"People who are between places live at motels or crash with friends."

"I was his friend."

"You were his meal ticket."

I shot him a glare, and he held up a hand to gesture for peace. "Alright, what was wrong with Barry?"

"Nothing was wrong with Barry," I said, in what had to be at least a slightly exasperated tone. Why couldn't we have had this conversation via text? It was so much easier to hide behind emojis. "He seems like a really nice guy."

Matt smiled. One of those Cheshire Cat smiles. "So... when are you seeing him again?"

"I don't know! We traded phone numbers. This goes two ways, you know, maybe he didn't like me."

"So, you like him?" He at least tried to cover his smile with a sip of cocoa this time.

Now I was the one that wanted to throw the pillow. How quickly the tables turn. "I didn't... not... like him. I mean, he was hot. I'll give you that. But looks aren't everything."

"I bet you two would make gorgeous babies."

"Shut up."

"Beautiful blond blue-eyed babies..."

"Argh!" The cocoa barely made it to the table before I pounced on him, knowing his particular weakness to tickle attacks.

We ended up in a tangled heap on the couch, breathless from laughing but content as kittens. Say what you will about Matt, but he gives good snuggles. A hand stroked my back, and I sighed, relaxing deeper while the television droned on quietly in the background. I hadn't even noticed what was on.

Matt was quiet for a few moments, but I felt him lift his head and press his lips into my hair. "Give him a chance," he said quietly, breath warm against my scalp. "Give someone a chance." There was a plea in there, not far from the surface.

"I'll try. I mean, he's nice. I had a good time. He's just…"

"Not me?"

Silence was the only answer I could muster. Sometimes the truth is hard to hear.

CHAPTER 4

I'm not sure quite what time it was when I fell into bed, but I knew exactly what time it was when my alarm went off the next morning. 5:00 a.m. I am not a morning person. That's why my alarm clock sat on my dresser across the room and not on my nightstand. After a minute or so of deciding that the pillow over my head wasn't drowning it out sufficiently—and I had about thirty seconds before the neighbor started banging on the wall—I crawled out from under the covers and just about froze my niblets off on the way across the room. The heat was out again. Fortunately, the hot water wasn't. I was soon showered, dressed, bundled up, and out the door, not even lingering for breakfast or coffee.

More snow had fallen overnight, but the road crews had been at work, and the streets were drivable. I arrived at the hospital in time to change into my scrubs and duck into the break room in search of sustenance.

"Ooooo... the breakfast gods shine upon me!" I exclaimed, upon catching sight of the box of bagels sitting on the table. I might have the occasional flair for the dramatic, especially on an empty stomach.

"Nothing but carbs," said the room's only other occupant. It was Gracie, one of the night-shifters, but the only thing she was nursing at the moment was a cup of coffee.

"Cream cheese isn't a carb." I grinned at her, then peeked inside and rummaged until I found an everything bagel near the bottom that had escaped the ravenous clutches of the carb-hungry horde. "Neither is lox, but that's probably too much to ask for free eats."

Gracie laughed. "Yeah, probably."

Although it was sacrilege, I opted to skip the toaster and grabbed a plastic knife, slathering on some schmear. "Oh hey, a Jane Doe came in yesterday. Weird case, she was comatose. Did anyone figure out who she is?" I asked, glancing over my shoulder briefly. Long enough to catch the look on Gracie's face. I knew the news wasn't good before she opened her mouth.

"Not that I know of, but... she coded. We couldn't bring her back. It was the strangest thing, though. She was perfectly healthy. All the labs and scans were normal, no indications of trauma..."

"Ugh, that sucks," I said, trying to sound more surprised than I actually was—which was not at all. A witch would rather die than live life without magic. My aforementioned cousin was a weak exception to the rule. At some point, no amount of medical care can give someone back the will to go on living.

Gracie carried her mug to the sink to rinse it out and departed, leaving me alone with my thoughts and my breakfast. I settled into a squishy chair and pretended to watch the television mounted on the wall.

My thoughts weren't on the news, or even the delicious bagel I was noshing. I kept thinking about Jane Doe. It was difficult to imagine losing something so important, so fundamental to your existence that you could simply die from losing the will to live without it. Sure, there are plenty of stories about old people who were married for decades, dying within days of each other. I'd seen it myself at a nursing home I did a clinical at during college. There wasn't any magic—or lack thereof—in that. Love makes messes of us all. I knew that all too well, but I guess I'd never loved someone so much that losing them made me want to throw in the metaphorical towel. Not even Matt. But I guess I didn't really lose him, did I?

Was losing the connection to magic like losing your soulmate? I'd met plenty of witches that seemed to be in love with themselves, but I wouldn't limit that trait to witchkind.

The bagel disappeared quickly, but in just enough time for me to start my shift. It seemed like reminders of the dead witch were everywhere. I'm no stranger to losing a patient. They almost always get to you in some way, but few really stick with you after the first year or so, especially given the volume at the ER. I saw dozens of patients on an average shift, and that day was no different. But every time I pulled that particular curtain aside, I half-expected to see her on the other side. Of course, she never was.

Where I did catch a glimpse of her now and then was on the television. Apparently, the police weren't having much luck figuring out who she was, which was actually kind of impressive given the size of Santa Fe. It's not a one-stoplight town or anything, but tourists aside, it was hard to be completely anonymous in a city of seventy thousand. Heck,

I'd recognized her, after all. However, if they were showing her photo on the news that meant that running her fingerprints didn't turn up anything. This told me three key pieces of information: she didn't have a driver's license, she'd never been arrested, and she wasn't a registered practitioner.

In the years since the truth about witches' existence came out, it'd been a rocky road. A lot of witches still kept their true nature hidden to avoid discrimination, prejudice, and other unpleasant consequences. The feds passed the buck on licensing to the states, which resulted in some pretty wide gaps in fees, requirements, and enforcement from state to state. In some states it was easier to buy a gun than get a license to practice magic. In New Mexico, all you had to do was register as a practitioner. There are plenty of witches here—and elsewhere—that don't want to be tracked in a government database. I can't say I blame them.

Anyway, not only was the Santa Fe Police Department working with a Jane Doe's mysterious death, they probably had no idea she had been a witch. They almost assuredly had no idea she had burned out before she died, and her witchy friends probably knew she was unregistered and didn't want to get her in trouble—or themselves, if they were also unregistered—so who knew if they'd report her missing, much less respond to her picture plastered across the six o'clock news.

I felt the weight of responsibility on my shoulders, and I didn't like it. Didn't like owing anything to those people. Witches had only ever caused me heartache. But if I didn't speak for the dead woman, who would? Resolved to seek out Jane Doe's people and break the bad news, I dropped by the cafe after work.

The Tin Whistle Cafe was a popular local haunt, and for

good reason. Its decor was best described as "rustic chic," spartan with long wood tables and metal chairs. But the work of local artists hung on the clean white walls and the food was amazing. It wasn't the sort of cafe that limited itself to coffee and muffins, not by a long shot. It just had a great vibe in general. It had become kind of a home away from home for me, and since I didn't really like to cook I was in there pretty regularly. Regularly enough that most of the employees knew me by name, anyway.

The patio outside was empty when I pulled into the parking lot, but that wasn't terribly surprising considering the tables under the folded umbrellas were covered in a good inch of snow. I loved sitting on the patio when the weather was nice, sipping java and people-watching or reading a book. But tonight wasn't a night for any of those things. Well, maybe the java.

I wasn't even sure if the witches would be there, but I had seen them there often enough that I felt it was a pretty safe bet. Stepping inside, I glanced around the room as I made my way to the counter to place my order. I spotted them as I stepped in line, two witches that I recognized as Jane Doe's friends—probably members of her coven—sitting at a table in the corner near the restrooms.

At a glance, I thought they might be lovers. He was Hispanic, mid-to-late thirties with the barest peppering of silver starting to show in his short black hair. She was younger, maybe around my age, with a natural ginger's pale complexion and a pixie-cut shock of light red hair. They sat across from one another, leaning across the table with fingers entwined. A faint glow of magic surrounded them, invisible to the mundane diners and staff around them. I didn't know what they were doing, but there was definitely energy gathered around them for whatever reason. It stopped as a server came by to drop off their food. They straightened in their seats, and the glow vanished as their hands broke contact. I looked away, studying the menu board behind the counter unnecessarily. Better that than being caught staring, right?

"Hey there, Emily, how's your night going?" The woman behind the counter had a shiny silver name tag reading "Penny". I always thought it was a little ironic, like they should have found her a copper one or something. I never mentioned it, because she probably got that a lot. I never claimed to be particularly original.

"Pretty good, thanks. Got a couple days off ahead of me to look forward to. How about you?"

"I'm good. Must be nice, Friday on Wednesday. What can I get you?"

I ordered a large latte with cinnamon. Penny paused, uncertain when I didn't order any food. "For here or to go?" she asked, with a slight tilt to her head. The downside of being a regular is that they start to notice your patterns, and while I might duck in during the day for a cup of coffee to go, if I came by in the evening it was usually for dinner.

"To go would be great, thanks." I smiled, hoping to convey it wasn't personal or anything while I slipped a hand in my pocket for my wallet.

Once the order was paid for, I moved on without making further social overtures. The evening rush was just getting started, as evidenced by the five or six people who had stepped into line behind me while I waited for my turn at the counter.

Taking a deep breath, I started to make my way across the bustling restaurant toward where the two witches were having dinner. I distracted myself from the unpleasant conversation to come by studying their plates as I approached. The gent had ordered a burrito slathered in green chile and cheese, while his companion was working her way through a plate of spring rolls with peanut noodles over greens. Salivating, I questioned my decision not to order dinner, but I had really wanted to make this a quick in and out.

From my angle of approach, it was the man who noticed me first. He paused in the act of cutting off another bite-sized chunk of burrito, brows lifting. I had no idea if he recognized me. I'd seen him plenty of times, but I had a good reason to notice him. He had no reason to notice me. I was just another mundie.

"Hey there, sorry to interrupt your meal. I just wanted to talk to you for a minute," I said. Straightforward and to the point. That was how I'd decided to approach the subject.

"Um, sure," he said. The woman sitting across from him twisted in her seat to look over at me curiously.

"I'm Emily. Emily Davenport." His brows went up again as soon as I said my last name. Shit. Remember how I said Davenport was a prestigious name? It's also a bit notorious in occult circles as one of the allied covens of the Circle, the self-appointed overseers of magical activity in North America. In short, they like to stick their noses in everyone's business, and they're powerful enough that no one can do anything about it. I rushed on. "I've seen you here before... Wow, that sounds unnecessarily creepy. But I think I saw your friend's picture on the news."

The man's face went passive again. He was good at hiding his thoughts, but I'd already seen his reaction to my name. "I don't know what you're talking about. What friend?"

I'm not a lie detector, but sometimes it's easier to see through bullshit than others. This time it was especially easy because I knew for a fact I had seen them together on more than one occasion.

"I'm not a cop or anything," I said. "I just thought maybe you'd like to know what happened to her."

His companion reached across the table and touched his arm. "Hector, she's one of us."

I blinked. What? I mean, sure, the name causes confusion now and then but I obviously wasn't a witch. Was she blind? Fortunately, Hector was looking across the table instead of at me. I darted a glance between them, catching a briefly uncomfortable look on Hector's face before he stood and politely asked the table next to us if he could borrow one of their chairs.

I should have corrected her. But if thinking I was a Davenport witch would get them to talk to me for a few minutes, well... I could fake it as long as they didn't ask about the secret witch handshake. (There isn't one. That I know of.)

So, instead of clearing up that gross misconception, I ignored the vague probability that my mother would reach across the miles and metaphysically bitch slap me and instead politely thanked Hector for getting me a chair and parked my ass in it.

"So," Hector said, resuming his seat and picking up his knife and fork again. He motioned with his fork for me to continue.

"Your friend—I'm sorry, I don't know her name. She was found downtown yesterday afternoon. She was brought to St. Vincent's because she was unresponsive, and she passed away late last night." Straight and to the point, right?

The female witch gasped, eyes widening. Hector set his knife and fork back down. I had a feeling they were going to end up taking their food to go, which was a shame because it looked really good.

"I told you something bad had happened," she said, her eyes filling with tears. "Why else would her picture be on TV?"

Hector didn't respond but to cover her hand with his while he stared me down.

"I'm sorry for your loss," I said. "But I thought you might know her family or something. The police weren't able to figure out who she was. She had no identification on her and she was," I lowered my voice, "unregistered."

Hector stiffened predictably and glanced around to assure himself that no one had overheard. "You ought to be more careful about how you say things like that," he replied, somewhat curtly.

I looked at his companion for help, but she was weeping softly. I'm not sure she'd even heard anything past the tragic news of her friend's passing.

"Um, I was being careful. It's not like I walked in here with a megaphone or something," I tossed back, maybe a little too caustically.

He grimaced but nodded slightly. "Victoria was a... very special woman."

"I'm sure she was. As I said, I'm sorry." I sat there awkwardly for a moment, wishing my coffee would arrive so I had something to do with my hands.

"You said she was unresponsive?" It was the woman who spoke this time, her voice soft, laced with fear or maybe just trepidation.

"Yes. I was there when she was brought in. I'm a..." I caught the significant look that the teary-eyed woman gave Hector, and I knew something was up; I just didn't know what. "...nurse."

Hector hesitated long enough that I broke the silence and awkward staring to ask, "What? What is it?"

The man grimaced distastefully and pushed his plate away. I was totally right about the need for a doggie bag. "We need to talk, but not here."

It was a good thing I'd ordered my coffee to go.

CHAPTER 5

Ginger Witch's name was Tracy. I learned this while they were trying to convince me to let them drive me wherever it was they wanted to go to see whatever it was they wanted me to see. I'm not an idiot. Well, not a total idiot. I drove myself out of town, then down that unlit dirt road to the double-wide trailer sitting on a snow-covered lot thick with brush. Letting the car idle for a moment, I fished my phone out of my pocket to send Matt a text and noticed I had several messages waiting for me. Apparently, I forgot to check my phone when I retrieved it from my locker at the end of my shift. Oops. Along with a few random messages from friends, I had a text from Barry.

Barry: Had a great time. We should get together again. Friday?

I couldn't help but smile. I hadn't completely scared him off, and it was a nice feeling to hear from him again so soon. I mean, a text that very night might have seemed a little eager, but the next day? Totally appropriate. A reply was going to require a little thought, and I didn't have time for that right then. Instead, I sent Matt a cryptic text that if he didn't hear from me in an hour to call the cops. I left my phone tucked under the floor mat too, just in case. It meant I couldn't call for help if I needed it, but Matt could use it to help the police find me if push came to shove. The "find phone" link between our phones was just one more tie we hadn't bothered to sever when we split up. Hell, I'm pretty sure I was still getting some of his mail.

I made a quick survey of my surroundings while I turned the car off and prepared to venture out into the cold once more. There were three other cars parked within eyesight. One was covered in snow and looked like it hadn't moved in a long time. The others had relatively fresh tracks leading to them and were more lightly dusted. The air smelled heavily of wood smoke. Out in the sticks, people relied even more on wood stoves and fireplaces for heat in the winter. Wondering what the big damn mystery was, I trudged through the snow to join Hector and Tracy where they waited for me by their truck. He had his arm around her shoulders, and she leaned against him, looking at the trailer with a worried expression. I began to get the feeling that while they might not have lured me out here for some sinister plot, whatever lay up the weathered front steps and behind that manufactured door wasn't something I'd enjoy. How'd I get myself into this mess, anyway? Oh right, some misplaced sense of moral obligation. I should probably see someone about that.

I approached them cautiously, hands in the pockets of my heavy winter coat. "Look, I feel like I've been a pretty good sport about this. What's going on?"

Hector didn't answer, turning instead to go up the wooden steps with a motion of his head for me to join him. Tracy shot me an apologetic look and went with him. At least it was clear who was calling the shots.

Swallowing a sigh, I glanced over my shoulder in the direction of my car before following them up to the tiny landing that didn't even really qualify as a porch. Hector knocked, and the door cracked open a few moments later. My view was blocked by the pair in front of me, but I thought I caught a glimpse of steely gray hair and one brown eye before the door closed again. I could hear the muffled rattle of a chain lock being unfastened. The door opened again, and Hector moved inside, followed by Tracy, and finally me, the unlikely caboose on this little mystery train.

The scent of incense washed over me, heavy in the air as I entered the dwelling. The floor creaked quietly under our feet in that way manufactured homes do, old enough that I was a little concerned that if I put my foot down too hard it might go right through the floor. It took my eyes a few moments to adjust to the change in light level. Outside, the sun was just getting around to setting, but inside it was already as dim as twilight. The windows were covered by woven blankets, and the only sources of light were a floor lamp and the television, which was turned down low. Two small children lay on the floor in front of the television, watching raptly as cartoon characters cavorted and sang. A wizened old woman sat in a rocking chair near the floor lamp, a smoking pipe between her yellowed teeth. Her hair was completely white, her brown skin wrinkled like an old prune. She stared at me for a long moment while Hector, Tracy, and the middle-aged man who had opened the door stood quietly, watching her for... something. I wasn't sure what, but I was suddenly very keenly aware that I was the only non-witch in the room. Even the children had that telltale spark. I stood there awkwardly, like an ant under a magnifying glass, trying not to fidget. After lengthy consideration, the old witch gave her head a little nod and went back to puffing her pipe. Whatever the test was, I guess I passed.

Hector turned to the man who had opened the door and said a few words in Spanish.

"Thank you for letting us come by, this won't take long." He glanced over his shoulder at me and I gave him a confused look. It wasn't much of a stretch, because I was pretty confused, just not about what he had said. But it's always interesting to hear what people have to say when they don't think you can understand them.

The older man seemed to wear a perpetual frown. He eyed me in a none-too-friendly fashion, but nodded to Hector and walked toward the kitchen, beyond which was a short hallway and a closed door.

Hector followed him, and Tracy shot me a supportive smile before following. I was starting to like her a little bit, but it'd probably pass. Left to bring up the rear again, I trailed quietly in their wake, looking around as I went. Though the house was humble in its appointments, it was well cared for and clean. The furniture was mismatched, the walls a faux-wood panel with various family photos, cheap art prints and children's drawings hanging on it. The kitchen sink was empty, with clean dishes drying in the drainer beside it. There was a battered old gas stove but nothing so luxurious as a dishwasher—which was a bare necessity as far as I was concerned. It was surprisingly tidy for a house with two small children in it, and I wondered if whoever kept it resorted to magical means to manage it more easily.

Down the hallway I went, but the closer I got to the door at the other end, the more the hair on my arms started to stand up—which is a pretty odd sensation when you're wearing a long sleeve shirt and a coat. I could sense magic, powerful magic, behind that door, but I couldn't see anything. It was strong enough that I felt like I should be seeing the glow of it through the crack between door and doorframe, but there wasn't anything there.

The older man opened the door and stepped into the room. As soon as he opened it, the glow from the next room nearly blinded me. I flung up a hand to shade my eyes and squinted into the sudden brightness, while ahead of me Hector and Tracy continued forward as if nothing were amiss.

My feet had halted when faced with the sudden glare, but I pressed onward again only to stop just before crossing the threshold into the room. The doorway was webbed with an intricate latticework of nearly invisible lines of power. They were blurry, like smudged residues of once-sharp images, and while I could recognize them as warding lines I wasn't at all certain what they were warding against. Hopefully not confused, in-over-their-head mundies, or I was in trouble.

My eyes began to adjust, and I lowered my hand to reach out and brush the near side of the ward with my fingertips. The lines of power flexed but didn't offer much in the way of resistance. My fingertips slipped through easily, and though it tingled a little it didn't hurt. A good thing, since I liked my fingertips as they were. Holding my breath, I stepped through the doorway and into the next room, which felt kind of like stepping through a cold spider web. It clung to me a little, and I shook myself on impulse on the other side, even though it'd already rebounded into place.

Hector, Tracy, and the older man were all standing there staring at me like I'd grown a third eye.

I cleared my throat softly and squared my shoulders, ignoring them as I took a few steps forward and looked around the room in the hope of seeing what it was that had brought me all the way out here. It wasn't just the doorway that was warded, but all four walls, the floor, and the ceiling. There was barely a square inch of paint or plaster visible anywhere in the room. Like the rest of the house, it was dim. Unlike the rest of the house, it was lit entirely with candles and an ancient-looking oil lamp, rather than any electrical source. I could imagine why. With this much magical energy lining the walls, it would disrupt any electrical current that tried to pass through it.

Also, like the rest of the house, the room was meticulously tidy, with everything in its place. My eyes were drawn to the conspicuous disruption to the order of the room. Namely, the lump under the covers on the otherwise meticulously made bed. A woman lay there, tucked under layers of woven blankets. Only her head and neck poked out from under them. She was bronze-skinned with dark hair parted down the center and plaited into thick braids that disappeared under the blankets. Her brown eyes were open, staring up at the ceiling much like Jane Doe's had; she lay there like an empty void in the center of a shimmering magical web, completely devoid of magic herself.

"Oh. Shit," I said. Sometimes I can be so damn eloquent.

Hector & Co must have recovered themselves by then because I heard a quiet click behind me of the door closing and then sensed a flare of power to my left. It was the only warning I got before a glowing spiderweb of power pushing a wall of air flung me backwards. I'm a little ashamed to admit that I squeaked in alarm, finding myself pinned against the back of the door that had just closed, pressed against the shimmering wards that seemed very aware of my presence. I felt them moving against my back, cold and alive. It was creepy.

"Hector!" Tracy's green eyes were wide as she lifted a hand to cover her mouth, looking on in alarm.

"Seconded!" I exclaimed, squirming to no avail. "What the fuck, man?" The magical bonds tightened, which only angered me further. I really hate it when people get the drop on me, and I'd walked right into this with the full knowledge that it might be a trap.

Hector stepped in front of me. "Where is he?" Even with him right in my face, it was difficult to focus on him with the amount of power he was wielding. He was either exceptionally gifted or in serious danger.

"Shit, calm down, man! I don't need another burned-out witch on my hands, and I don't know what you're talking about!"

"Who are you, really? Did he send you?" He stepped even closer. I could smell green chile on his breath. It wasn't super pleasant, second-hand.

"I don't know who you're talking about. I told you who I am. My name is Emily. I'm a nurse at St. Vincent's. I treated your friend. Victoria, right?" I was getting desperate, and I looked over at Tracy for help, but she just stood there with her hand over her mouth. Power flared around her a moment later, and I hoped that meant she was prepared to step in if she needed to. But even the presence of a potential ally made me angrier. I hate feeling helpless, and this situation was a keen reminder of just how powerless I was in the face of this sort of opposition.

"You're not a Davenport," Hector insisted, and I think his eyes narrowed, but I was getting a little dizzy. Why the hell did I give them my last name? I must not have answered fast enough, because he started rifling my pockets until he found my wallet, then started pulling shit out of it and letting it all sift down to the clean floor like so much detritus.

When he found my driver's license, he frowned as he studied it, then held it up to compare the terrible DMV photo against my actual face. Fortunately, there was enough resemblance for verification. The spiderweb of power securing me to the wall ghosted away, and I slid down the door a few inches until my feet made contact with the floor again. I stumbled forward and landed on my hands and knees, just trying to get away from the discomfort of the wards at my back.

"You know," I said after a moment, lifting my head to shoot a small glare up at him, emboldened because the glow around him had faded. "If you'd just asked to see that to start with, you could have saved yourself some embarrassment."

CHAPTER 6

I couldn't get out of that house fast enough. Away from Hector, away from the burned-out witch in her magical tomb, away from the children quietly glued to the television set and the cloying scent of incense and tobacco smoke. No one tried to stop me, but Hector and Tracy followed me outside, the former calling thanks and apologies to the hosts for the "rude white bitch" in Spanish on the way out.

That didn't do much for my already-flared temper, let me tell you.

It wasn't until I was halfway to the car that he tried to stop me, reaching out to catch hold of my arm. This time I was ready, and instead of pulling away from him I balled up a fist and twisted, bringing my fist upward in a stiff uppercut that landed squarely on his jaw. His head rocked back, and he released me instantly. Tracy cried out in alarm, magic flaring around her as she rushed to him. I tensed, but she wasn't paying me any attention. No, she reached up to touch his face, probably mending whatever minimal damage I had done.

Backing up, still angling in the direction of my parked

car, I shook my hand out. Punching someone hurts, but sometimes I just can't help myself.

Hector brushed Tracy off once she was finished, brow furrowed as he focused his attention on me. "Where do you think you're going?" He was clearly not as finished with the conversation as I wanted to be.

"Wherever the hell I want!" I retorted, gloved fingers fumbling for my car keys around all the junk now loose in my coat pocket. "Away from here, that's for damned sure. Where do you get off, anyway? I don't know who the hell you're looking for, but I don't have anything to do with any of this. I'm just a nurse." I jammed my thumb down on the remote entry button, and the driver's door unlocked behind me.

"Daniel Davenport," he said.

The name gave me pause. Enough pause that he smirked and folded his arms.

"So you do know him," he said. That telltale glow came alive around him again, and I responded by yanking the car door open and trying to dive inside before he could sling another spell at me. It's a lot harder to cast magic through a hunk of glass and metal. Not impossible, but harder. I almost made it, but a rope of power coiled around my foot and dragged me back out the open door and across the snow toward where the witches stood.

I was getting really tired of being magically manhandled by this asshole. "Goddammit! Quit that!" I grabbed at the snowy ground but found no purchase. My gloved fingers left furrows in the snow as I slid backward until he stopped pulling.

"Just tell us where to find him, and we'll let you go!" Tracy finally spoke again, but I wasn't sure if I could trust Hector to honor the offer.

I glared over my shoulder at both of them. "I haven't heard from him in years. I don't know where he is. Assuming the Daniel Davenport I know is even the one you're looking for."

"Awfully big coincidence, two Davenport witches showing up in Santa Fe at the same time, isn't it?" Hector challenged.

I glared at him some more. "If I was a Davenport witch you'd be strung up from a tree by your short and curlies right now, buddy. I told you, I'm a nurse. I've been here for years. Hell, I'm a regular at the cafe. That's how I found you in the first place."

"But you could see the wards. If you're not a witch, what are you?" Tracy asked, her confusion clear.

I gave a mighty tug against Hector's mystical tentacle, my overactive imagination half expecting it to start creeping up my leg like some sort of Japanese schoolgirl hentai nightmare. But he released me, and I rolled over, pushing myself up to sit on my ass at their feet. "Witch Lite? Tastes great, less filling? I'm a null. I don't have any power. I never did. I don't even know what those wards in there are warding off. Wait, now that you mention it, what are they warding off?" I frowned up at him, but it was Tracy who spoke up this time.

"They're protections, preventing further harm from coming to Christina. They keep magic, magical creatures, constructs, and magic users—except for those attuned to them, anyway—from passing through them into the room. We expected them to stop you, but they didn't," she explained, earning a glare from Hector, but she stood her ground.

Well, that certainly explained the way they were looking at me when I jumped that particular shark. "Okay," I said.

"Now, what the hell does my little brother have to do with two burned-out witches in the ass crack of New Mexico?"

"That's what we'd like to ask him," Hector said grimly. "He was... 'friendly' with them both. And now all of a sudden they've both burned out. Tori is dead, and Christina might as well be. Joseph—Christina's husband—is out for blood. We just want to find him before Joseph does. Get some answers."

Suddenly it all started to make a strange sort of sense. "Okay, that does sound like Dan. The friendliness, I mean. Dan's very friendly." Sticking his dick where it probably didn't belong had become his specialty, or so I'd heard through the grapevine.

I started to pick myself up off the ground. "If you touch me with magic again I'm going to start screaming 'stranger danger' at the top of my lungs," I cautioned, brushing snow from my pant legs. He said nothing, so I took that silence as assent. "I don't know where Dan is, but I'll try to track him down. I doubt he had anything to do with what happened to your friends. He's not evil, he's just... morally challenged."

"How do I know you won't help him escape?" Hector asked, frowning hard enough that I could hear it in his voice.

"I guess you'll have to take my word for it."

"Why would I do that?"

"I don't even know where to start... but, okay." I ticked the points off on my fingers. "One, I came to you voluntarily with information out of the kindness of my fucking heart, and I like to think I've been a pretty good sport about you batting me around like a cat with a ball of yarn. Two, if I'd known Dan was sleeping his way through your coven I wouldn't have given you a reason to link me to him. Hell, I probably would have just left an anonymous note on your car. Three, if Dan wasn't involved—whether you like it or not—he could be the best bet you have to figure out what happened."

Hector had too much pride to accept that last one without a fight, but I didn't expect otherwise. He puffed up like a challenged rooster, opening his mouth to crow a protest but closing it when I held up a hand.

"You two can wave your metaphysical dicks at each other in person. I'm not getting involved. But there's a reason you reacted to the Davenport name. You know who they are, and you know what they can do. He may be an ass, but he's a well-trained ass. If anyone can figure out what happened to your friends, he probably can." I backtracked to my car. Once I got there, I had to rummage for my keys a bit, because I'd dropped them inside somewhere when I'd been unceremoniously dragged off by the ankle.

"Alright, I'll let you go on one condition," he said.

I poked my head out of the car. "What's that?"

"Leave me something personal so I can find you. A talisman."

"Orrrrr I could give you my phone number and you can call me." I tried not to sound sarcastic, but that's never been my forte.

Witches. Always wanting to do things the hard way.

CHAPTER 7

It was nearly 9 p.m. when I finally stumbled into my dark apartment, fumbling for a light switch as I fended off the advances of the four-legged furball that was until that moment convinced I was never going to come home and feed him. Purring noisily, he flung himself against my ankles in a display of affection that wasn't fooling me in the slightest; once he was fed he'd go back to ignoring me as usual.

Barrington—or "Lord" Barrington, as Matt called him—rarely lowered himself to hobnobbing with the servants. He was a big fluffy orange tabby with one blue eye and one green eye, which was unnerving when he took to staring at you, but it was cute when he was a kitten. That's my only excuse for adopting him from the shelter; he was just so damn cute, and I needed something cute and fluffy in my life in the wake of the awkward end of my romantic relationship with Matt. Little did I know, Barrington would grow up into a lazy beast that shunned social interactions most of the time in favor of lying in sunbeams and in front of doors that needed to be opened. Oh, and hacking up the occasional monster hairball.

The cat got fed before I did, a scoop of dry kibble added to his bowl before I contemplated the slim pickings in my fridge. "Sandwich it is," I said to the empty kitchen and set to making one. The blossom of color on my right hand drew my attention while I worked. The knuckles were bruising up nicely from the contact they'd made with Hector's face. At least I hadn't split any of them the way I had that time I punched my sister—but that's a story for another time. Let's just say she had it coming, and growing up Davenport wasn't easy for a null. Throw in raging teenage hormones, and I was basically a ticking time bomb for a few years.

The sandwich went into the bathroom with me, because it had been a long day, the heat still wasn't working, and I wanted nothing quite so much as a long, hot bath. My bathtub wasn't anything fancy, but it was big enough that I could settle down into the water and be mostly covered. Being able to do that was a luxury I never took for granted; I learned how to numb myself with food at a young age. I'd been a chunky kid growing up—like my slim, gifted siblings needed anything else to tease me about. But during nursing school, I buckled down and lost the extra weight. I wish I could say I was one of those people who didn't have to work at maintaining a healthy weight. If I wasn't careful, the pounds would start creeping on again. But I watched what I ate most of the time and exercised, even though I'd never reached the point where I actually enjoyed it.

Once I finished my sandwich and was down to simply soaking among the bubbles, I reached for my phone and called Matt, leaving the phone on speaker on the edge of the tub.

"So, what was that all about?" he asked as soon as he picked up. Not even a hello. I'd called him on the way home to let him know I was safe, but he was expecting a bit more detail. So I filled him in on what happened with Jane Doe (aka Victoria Young) and the events of the evening right up to and including my little brother's presence in Santa Fe and the coven's suspicions about him being involved in the incidents that left two of their number burned out.

Matt is the only person I've ever told the full truth about my family, though it ceased to be top secret when witches came out of the broom closet five years ago. My reluctance to share it was more instinct and self-defense than anything. I just wanted to be normal. That's why I moved across the country to begin with, to live a normal life without all the baggage that came with being a Davenport, a woman without magic from a long line of witches with more than their share. Tonight was just an unpleasant reminder that I'd probably never be truly free of it.

"Maybe I should change my name," I said with a sigh, playing with a little pile of bubbles. I'd mound them up and then sweep them under the water, watching them float to the surface again.

"You can't hide forever. Things have a way of creeping up on you, regardless." He was right. Tonight was certainly evidence of that.

"Speaking of hiding, I need tech support." Matt was a tech guru in addition to a culinary genius, one of those cute brainy guys that seemed to know everything about anything electronic. He worked in IT, so that was a good trait.

"Oh, I can't wait to hear this. Did you use your cd tray as a coffee holder?"

"Ha. Ha. 1995 called. It wants its joke back." I've never done that, I swear. My laptop doesn't even have a cd tray. "But seriously, I need to know how to turn off caller ID on my phone, so I can make one of those calls that comes up as 'unknown number' on the other end."

"Oh, that's easy. Dial star sixty-seven before you dial the number. Why? Gonna call Barry and heavy breathe at him?"

I sat up suddenly, nearly sloshing water over the edge of the tub where my phone was sitting. "Oh, shit! He texted me today, and I was going to text him back, but then I was derailed by angry witches."

Matt laughed, and we chatted a few more minutes about inconsequential things before hanging up so I could make my next call.

I didn't have the hotline number for Jane Doe handy, so I looked up the non-emergency line for the police department and dialed it. Two rings later, a husky-voiced woman picked up.

"Santa Fe Police Department, this is Darcy. How can I help?" Darcy sounded bored. I'll bet the non-emergency line is a lot less exciting than 911.

"I'd like to report some information about that woman, the Jane Doe whose picture has been on the news."

There was a flutter of keyboard tapping in the background, then, "May I have your name please?"

"No," I said, perhaps a little too quickly. "I'd like to remain anonymous."

"Okay, what would you like to report?"

"Her name is Victoria Young, and she was an unregistered witch." I could tell my words were being recorded verbatim by the rapid staccato of Darcy's typing. There was a pause, to give me a chance to say more.

"That's it," I said and hung up.

My heart was thumping fast as I sat there trying to remember how long it took to trace a call. It was something like thirty seconds, right? I really should have set a timer or something. Hindsight.

The water was starting to get tepid, but I had one more

call to make. Or text to make. It's better to call someone when you apparently ignored their text for eight-plus hours, right? But by then it was almost 10 p.m., so... text it was. But what to say? I didn't want to seem too eager. Or too disinterested, especially after the long delay in answering. Therefore, I started off with "Sorry" but didn't get any further because a sudden movement in the corner of my eye gave me a start—maybe I was still a little jumpy after all the magic that was thrown at me that night—and the phone slid from my hands to land with a plop in the water.

"Shit!" I tried to prioritize the three immediate impulses that vied for my attention; sitting up, finding my phone with a quickness, and investigating what the movement was. My cat had suddenly materialized on the toilet seat—not via teleportation, but in the mundane but stealthy manner of an ordinary house cat. While I was flailing around in the tub trying to fish out my phone and generally get over my surprise and alarm, he sat there staring at me with his mismatched eyes like I was the strangest creature he'd ever encountered.

Ah-ha! My fingers finally closed on the phone, and I rescued it from the drink, held it aloft and watched it drip with dismay. "Great, just great," I muttered, climbing out of the tub and feeling no guilt at all about flicking water at Barrington to get him to move his furry ass off my towel. Predictably, he beat a hasty retreat.

Despite the chill in the air, I dried the phone off first. Standing naked beside the tub, shivering and dripping onto the bathmat, I folded it in the towel and pressed from both sides, like that might somehow squeeze the water out of the innards. Once it was as dry as I could get it, I set it on the counter and dried myself off quickly before donning the sweatpants, tank top, and sweater that I'd brought in with me. I wasn't sure if I should even touch a button to see if it was okay, or if trying to activate it right now might just make things worse.

I drained the tub and brought the phone out into the living room, grabbed my laptop, and settled on the couch with both.

The email I hastily fired off to Matt had one word in the subject line: HELP.

CHAPTER 8

I felt like an idiot walking into a ski resort holding a cell phone in a ziplock bag full of rice. I tried to think of it as penance for my idiocy the previous night. I wasn't sure if Matt was just messing with me or what, but I did what he had instructed anyway. It couldn't make anything worse, at that point. Fortunately, even as bare as my cupboards tended to be, I did have half a box of that quick-cooking rice. I'm pretty sure it's law in New Mexico that all homes must contain rice and green chile. Rice, I can cook. Green chile? No idea. Hopefully, the compliance officer had a thing for blondes.

The looks I received ranged from confused to amused as I walked through the well-appointed lobby with my head held high. I wasn't exactly dressed for fun on the slopes, and I didn't have any luggage with me, so I'm sure people were wondering what sort of business I had at the resort. Bypassing the front desk, I walked to the back of the lobby, past the elevators and down the hallway that terminated with a locked door sporting an "Employees Only" sign. Ordinarily, I'd text Matt to let him know I was there, and he'd let me in. Today, I had to use the callbox above the keycard reader. There was no answer to the first press of the button, so I leaned on it a little extra long the second time.

"Yeah?" The voice over the speaker was male and sounded like it was spoken in a big empty box.

"I'm here to see Matt Andrews. He's expecting me."

"Name?"

"Emily Davenport."

I waited while he did whatever it was he needed to do to verify me and pulled open the door when the buzzer sounded. The well-lit hallway beyond was lined with doors leading to various offices, but right inside the door was the security office with its big glass window. I waved to the man inside, who despite knowing he had just buzzed me in was in the process of taking a bite of a huge breakfast burrito.

I stepped into the doorway and leaned casually against the doorframe, jiggling my bag of rice. "I know the way, I just need a temp badge," I offered, helpfully. But protocol was protocol, and I had to jump through all the usual hoops to sign in formally before he walked me down the hall to Matt's office. The door was open, and inside the room, Matt swiveled in his chair to greet me with a smile.

"Hey Em! Thanks for walking her back, Brad."

The security guard nodded and, his due diligence done, headed back down the hall to finish his breakfast.

Matt's office wasn't the dark cave of the stereotypical geek. It was an interior room, so obviously there were no windows. But the stark fluorescent lighting was a far cry from bioluminescent mushrooms. The room was spacious enough for a large desk as well as a workbench, the surface of both workspaces tidy with a place for everything and everything in its place. There wasn't a notepad or post-it note to be seen anywhere—Matt was very much a digital guy. If it needed doing, he had an app for it.

Instead of those annoying motivational posters corporate America is so fond of, he had a cheeky selection of framed "demotivational" posters on the walls. My personal favorite had always been "Cluelessness. There are no stupid questions, but there are a lot of inquisitive idiots." I felt like one of those idiots walking into Matt's office with my cell phone in a baggie of rice.

"Your patient, doctor." I couldn't help the sheepishness that crept into my voice as I drifted farther into the room and held the baggie out to him.

"Thank you, nurse," he replied with a wink. "Let's get it to the OR, stat." It was funny because I really was a nurse, get it? Maybe you had to be there. Regardless, I laughed and followed him to the workbench, where he extracted my phone from the baggie and set it down on the anti-static mat. "Still in the case, eh?"

"You didn't tell me to take it out! Shit, is that bad?"

"Not necessarily. It could have kept some of the water out. I keep telling you to get one of those life-proof ones. I can get you a good deal on one. I know a guy."

"Yeah, I know. They're just so bulky. Part of the cool factor of having one of these things is that they're so slim and light." I leaned against the workbench and watched as he removed the phone from its case and studied the device from a few angles before grabbing a tiny screwdriver from where it hung with the rest of its set on the wall. I don't know how he managed to get the right size on the first try. Maybe it was luck.

"Do you do this a lot?" I wondered, still watching him work.

"With phones? Not really. But you'd be surprised how much coffee gets spilled into keyboards around here."

I winced. "Man, and I thought bedpan duty was bad."

Laughing and shaking his head, he finished with the screws, lining them all up in a pattern on the mat that matched where he had taken them out of the phone. It took him a minute to figure out how the case itself opened, but he soon had it in two pieces so he could inspect the interior.

"So," I said, quickly growing bored of watching him poke around in the waterlogged guts of my cell phone, "I was thinking as long as I'm here maybe you could help me with something else."

"Hmm?"

"Well, I need to find Dan and there aren't a ton of places locally that I can imagine a rich playboy staying. It's not like Santa Fe has a bunch of luxury hotels, so I figure he's either staying here or at one of the casinos."

"He could have rented a house."

I snorted. "From what I've heard, that's far too practical for my baby brother. Anyway, it seems like it wouldn't be too hard for you to find out if he's staying here..."

Matt paused his work to glance over at me, eyeing me with a faint smirk. "What's in it for me?"

"Pleeeeeeease?" I batted my lashes and used my best wheedling tone. "I'll love you forever."

"You'll love me forever anyway."

"I'll make you dinner."

"I'd do it if you promised *not* to make me dinner, maybe."

"I'll buy you dinner?"

He considered this offer, eyes dropping back down to the phone he was working on cleaning with some sort of alcohol-smelling solution from a tiny squeeze bottle and cotton swabs. "Dinner and dancing?" As counter-offers go, it wasn't too shabby. I'd happily do both with him pretty much anytime.

"Done."

In the end, I struck out on both fronts. The phone was a loss, and there weren't any Davenports in the resort's guest database at all. Matt walked me to the security desk, where Brad the security guard collected my temp badge and signed me out before sending me on my way.

"Don't forget!" Matt called down the hall to me as he walked backward in the direction of his office. I must have given him a confused look because he lifted his arms as if dancing with an invisible partner and boogied his way a few steps down the hall. I couldn't help but laugh, nodding and waving to him on my way out the door.

Walking across the snow-covered resort's huge courtyard, I pondered the dilemma of tracking down my brother. For the first time in a decade, I came close to regretting cutting ties with my family when I left home. To say that I was estranged from my family might be an understatement. When I left for college, I may have said a few things that earned me the "ungrateful" tag as well as the "disappointing" one. My youthful rage has faded a bit since then, or maybe just matured into bitter spite. I can still be angry about it all if I let myself, but one of the things I've learned in life is that if you spend too much time focusing on what makes you angry, sad, or frustrated there's no time left for anything else.

The only family member I was still in contact with at all was my older brother, Liam. Liam, as it turned out, became a disappointment to our mother in a whole other way; he's gay. Now, don't get me wrong. My best friend is queer. I've got nothing against the gays. My parents weren't homophobes either. But they had this thing about carrying on the bloodline, and they were old-fashioned enough to place a bit of pressure on their eldest to do it. Fortunately, science has progressed to the point that being straight—or at least willing to copulate with a member of the opposite sex—isn't a prerequisite for fathering a child. Liam and his husband want kids, but they haven't quite worked out the logistics of surrogacy just yet.

In any case, Liam contacted me a few years back and apologized for being such an ass when he was younger. I think he came to understand a little bit of the alienation I felt, in his own way, when he came out. I'm not saying we became besties, but we did communicate a few times a year after that. He got in the habit of sending me updates on what's going on in the family around the holidays, pictures of our sister's growing brood, stuff like that. I didn't really care, but it was a nice gesture.

If anyone could get me in touch with Dan, it was Liam. But in order to get in touch with Liam, I had to get my phone situation resolved.

I'm not sure how many times he called my name before it penetrated the fog of my distraction. Turning my head, I squinted into the midday sun reflecting off all the snow, shielding my eyes. A tall figure in a black and green ski suit was walking toward me, waving a hand. It took me a few moments to recognize Barry in his "work clothes."

This could be awkward.

"Barry! Hey!" I waited while he finished his approach and flashed him a deeply apologetic look. "I'm so sorry I didn't answer your text. I forgot to check my phone at the end of my shift and then..." I still had my phone, once more in the bag of rice. I held it up for him to see. "I had a little accident."

Wincing, he nodded. "Yeah, Matt mentioned it. That really sucks. I guess he wasn't able to fix it?"

Of course Matt mentioned it. Why couldn't I find a nice mundane guy that at least didn't start out in cahoots with my bestie?

"Nope." I shrugged. "Next stop, retail therapy. I'm going to have to get a new one. I know it's not the end of the world, but I feel so naked without my phone."

"Yeah, I know how that is. Hey, my roommate's band is playing a gig this weekend if you're interested in coming out. I could give you a tour backstage, buy you a drink?"

"When is it?" I asked, biting my lip.

"Um, if you've got plans, that's okay. I just thought I'd offer. It's Friday night at eight."

Quick to smile, I shook my head. "No, it's not that at all. I have to work Saturday, but tomorrow night should be fine as long as you don't keep me out too late. I'd like that. Email me the info? I'll give you my address." He passed me his phone and I put my address into it for him before handing it back with a smile.

"See you tomorrow, then?" he asked, grinning boyishly. It was charming, I have to admit.

"See you then."

CHAPTER 9

I went straight from the resort to the store to pick up a new phone. You don't really think about how much you rely on something like that until you don't have one anymore. I felt blind and deaf. It hadn't even been twenty-four hours. It's not like I'm a social butterfly, but it's nice to be connected to the people you care about. And, sometimes, the ones you don't. I hoped Hector hadn't tried to reach me, or I was going to be eating some serious crow.

The new phone was considerably flashier than the old one. Truth be told, I was overdue for an upgrade anyway. I stopped off at home for lunch and to sync the new phone with my laptop.

I had a bunch of things I'd planned to do that day, it being my day off and all, but I began to doubt I'd get any of them done. Most of them had been supplanted by one crucial task: find Dan.

I started by calling each of the local casinos. There aren't any in Santa Fe proper, but if you go a little bit north of town there are a few. Unfortunately, none of them were willing to page the casino floor for a guest, and of course the ones that also had resorts attached wouldn't tell me if they had any Davenports in residence. I didn't even try; that was more of an in-person sort of thing, when I could at least flash my ID and play the family card. I'd just have to start with the closest one and work my way out.

Before I left, I called Liam. His voicemail picked up quickly, so he was probably on the line already.

"Hey Liam, it's Emily. Could you text me Dan's number? It's important. Thanks."

Short and to the point, that's me. He'd have questions, but I had shit to do. Namely, slipping into something a little less comfortable.

I'm not one of those women who takes forever to change clothes and "put on her face," so within about fifteen minutes I was ready to head out. Taking a last look in the mirror on the back of my bedroom door, I tilted my head and turned a little, inspecting the goods.

"Not bad, Em..." I'm not really prone to talking to myself all that often, but there wasn't anyone else around to admire my handiwork at the moment. I'd picked out a pair of black skinny jeans and a tailored blouse, the darts along the torso accentuating my curves. I had the sleeves partway rolled up and an extra button undone to great effect. If I did say so, myself. One of my favorite turquoise pendants on a thin silver chain drew the eyes naturally down the V neck of my shirt, which I thought would serve me well with the front desk clerks. I wore my shoulder-length blond hair down, and a few quick twists of the curling iron had given it a little texture. I'd used some light base to cover the freckles on my face and went a little heavy with the eyeliner to give my boring brown eyes a little more drama. A touch of lipstick was all I'd needed to finish it.

My phone had been conspicuously silent the whole

time. I thumbed the home button on my way down the hall, but there were no new messages. Well, at least I hadn't gotten all dolled-up for nothing. Grabbing my coat and keys, I headed out to start the search in earnest.

The Camel Rock Casino was just a few miles up Highway 285 north of Santa Fe, one of a dozen or so tribal-run casinos in New Mexico. It was owned and operated by the Tesuque Pueblo and named after a distinctive rock formation easily visible on the other side of the highway. The Tesuque Pueblo dates back to the 13th century CE as a settlement, though the Tesuque people themselves didn't settle there until the 17th century.

How does a white girl from Boston know so much about local native history? Because I gave a shit and looked it up. It's fascinating, at least to me. But history was always one of my favorite subjects, so maybe I'm a little biased.

What Camel Rock didn't have was a hotel on the premises, so my front desk schmoozing would have to wait for the next stop. Walking onto a casino floor was always a little jarring. The lights, the sounds, the smells, it can be overwhelming if you're not expecting it. I'd been there before, once or twice, but gambling wasn't my thing. It felt like throwing perfectly good money away, but maybe that's because I wasn't good at it, and I didn't have a ton of extra cash to burn. There are the pure chance games, of course, but those are heavily weighted in the house's favor.

The air was thick with magic, anti-cheating and anti-tampering wards on every machine and table. High up on one wall were a long bank of mirrors that I suspected were actually one-way windows. I imagined a room full of video screens behind them, being watched by mundane security specialists while stony-faced witches watched the floor directly for signs of magic use that would distort the video image and make it difficult to see what was going on. It wasn't just bad form to cast spells in a casino. It could get you thrown out. The particularly hardcore establishments would stop anyone on the way in that had any type of active spell or charm on them, refusing them entry unless they dispelled it.

I decided to start in the bar, not knowing what sort of games Dan would most likely be playing. My eyes scanned the tables as I strolled into the bar, looking for a familiar face and wishing I'd thought to look for a recent photo of him in one of Liam's emails before I left, or at least took the time to set up the mail app on my phone so I could now. Dan was fourteen years old the last time I saw him in the flesh, but I was sure I'd still recognize him if I saw him.

I tried not to make eye contact with anyone as I scanned the room, but couldn't entirely avoid it. Once or twice, I got an inquisitive smile for my trouble. I made it a point not to smile back. No reason to be overly encouraging. Ending up at the bar, I lifted a hand to get the bartender's attention. Always best to order a drink before someone tries to buy one for you. Nothing in this world is ever really free.

"Ginger ale, please," I said to the bartender when she finished up the customer she was pouring for and wandered down to help me. She had that chiseled jaw and dark hair/eyes so common to Native Americans. On her, it was more handsome than beautiful.

"Opening a tab, sweetie?" she asked, and her voice was much deeper than I expected.

"No thanks," I answered, fishing out my wallet to hand over my credit card. While my drink was poured, I was completely distracted trying to figure out if the bartender was a man or a woman. They just had this total androgyny thing going on. It was fascinating, and that's probably why I didn't pay any particular notice to the man in the brown leather jacket slipping up to the bar beside me until he spoke.

"Excuse me."

I turned, looking over at him with a polite refusal of whatever it was he wanted ready on my lips. But it wasn't me he was talking to. It was the bartender.

"Be right with you," they said, setting my drink on a napkin in front of me. There were two cherries impaled on a tiny plastic sword floating in there with the ice. Nice touch.

The man beside me nodded and looked up at the television over the bar, watching the football game that was playing while he waited. He appeared to be in his thirties, with laugh lines framing his mouth and a full head of short dark hair. He wore a button-up shirt and jeans under his leather jacket, and a necktie was askew beneath his collar. I couldn't quite tell if he was Hispanic or Native American, which could be problematic in this region. Much like the bartender, he had a chiseled jaw, but he also had a neatly trimmed mustache riding his upper lip. Native American men tend to prefer being clean-shaven. It's a common misconception, as a result, that they can't grow facial hair. Random trivia. You're welcome.

The bartender returned with my credit card slip and card, sliding them across the bar to me. I thanked them before they turned to the man next to me.

"What can I get you?"

I was barely paying attention at this point, busy signing for my eight-dollar (?!) drink and making a mental note to keep the receipt. When this mess was dealt with, maybe Dan would reimburse me for my trouble.

When I looked up again, the man beside me had placed a photograph on the bar and was sliding it across toward the bartender. It was one of those grainy security camera still frames, and difficult to process upside down, but I watched curiously while the bartender picked it up and looked at it before shaking their head and sliding it back. This time it was right side up, and I glanced at it again, choking on my drink as my brain processed the image of Victoria, very much alive and animated, walking into this very casino on the arm of one Daniel Davenport.

I set my drink down quickly, covering my mouth with the other hand while I coughed a few times. Both the bartender and the man beside me glanced over at me. Heck, the guy even thumped me on the back helpfully.

"You okay?" he asked.

"Yeah... sorry... wrong pipe," I managed to choke out, reaching for a napkin to wipe some of the sugary liquid I'd suddenly spit out from my face. He eyed me briefly, then turned his attention back to the bartender.

"If you remember something later..." He pulled a little business card wallet from his jacket pocket and offered his card. I wasn't able to get a good look at it, but the bartender pocketed it before heading off to take care of another customer.

Me, well, I recovered what scraps of dignity I could and sipped my drink again, trying to clear my throat.

"Are you sure you're okay?" The man asked, looking over at me as he tucked the photo back into an inner jacket pocket. I assured him I was fine, and he nodded before moving off toward the casino floor.

When I could breathe again, I took a really deep breath and let it out slowly before turning from the bar with the rest of my drink in hand. If Dan was here, the stakes had just gone up. I was pretty sure I'd just met the jilted husband that wanted to kill him.

CHAPTER 10

I wasn't sure what direction the man from the bar had gone when he left. I glanced around as I exited but didn't see him anywhere. Not a surprise, really. Casinos are great places to disappear even if you aren't trying. Hopefully, that worked in my favor too. I attempted to melt into the crowd, moving past the machine gaming area and in the direction of the dealer-manned tables. I didn't know if Dan was a slots or video poker kind of guy, but if I were a betting woman, I know where my money'd be. You can't charm a machine, so he'd probably stick to games with a human dealer.

My eyes skimmed the crowd, skipping anyone that didn't have that telltale magical signature of a witch. There were only a dozen or so of them in this part of the gaming floor, and I managed to rule a number of them out by gender. If Dan had become Danielle, I'm pretty sure Liam would have mentioned it. Then again, maybe it had been in one of those holiday updates I hadn't read. If I hadn't seen that photo in the bar I'd have way more cause for concern.

I sipped my drink as I moved from table to table until I

finally caught sight of my blond-haired younger brother playing blackjack and flirting with an older woman wearing enough jewelry that it was a wonder she could hold herself upright. There wasn't a trace of gray in her brown hair, but the lines on her face belied an otherwise carefully cultivated youthful couture. As for Dan, well, he looked pretty much the same as the picture except in living color rather than black and white. His blond hair was just short of falling in his eyes, and his brown eyes were warm and sparkling with humor and mischief. He was wearing a pair of slacks and a turtleneck, clean-shaven and hale. I admit, part of me had wondered if he had run into the same trouble his paramours had. Fortunately, the evidence was to the contrary; that spark of magic was still alive and well in him.

"There you are!" I said as I approached, gaining at least a little smug satisfaction when Dan turned and looked at me blankly for a moment before he recognized me.

"Emily! Hey!" He flashed me a boyish grin and turned from the table to greet me.

"Daniel," I said, stepping forward to give him a hug and a brief kiss on the cheek. I wasn't feeling particularly warm toward this reunion, but it gave me a chance to get close enough to murmur, "We need to go. Now."

If Dan was surprised by the manner of greeting, he hid it well. "Oh, come on. I'm on a hot streak here thanks to my lucky charm." His eyes roved to the cougar on his right, and he smiled charmingly at her. She smiled back, toying with the straw in her drink.

I smiled, though I'm sure the sentiment didn't quite reach my eyes, and set my drink down on the table. "Sorry," I said to the older woman, raking Dan's chips off the table and shoving the tray at him. "Time to cash out."

I grabbed his arm and all but bodily hauled him from

the table. He went along without much more than a token protest, obviously having no care for the urgency I sought to convey.

"What are you doing in this neck of the woods?" he asked while we made our way to the cashier's window.

"Looking for you, dumbass."

"Now that's the charming sister I remember," he teased, still grinning like this was a great game to him. I glanced over at him and caught him making eyes at a young brunette in passing. "But really—"

He didn't get any further, because I saw the man in the leather jacket heading our way. Grabbing Dan, I turned and put my back against a nearby pillar, pulling him close so his back was to the man about to pass nearby.

"Look, I'm not saying you aren't totally smokin' but I'm not a 'keep it in the family' kind of guy," Dan said, still wearing that careless grin.

I wanted to slap him. Instead, I glared at him and reached up to take his head between my hands. I tried to make it look to passers-by that I wanted to kiss him rather than pop his head off, but it was tough. "There's a man here showing your picture around. A picture of you with a dead witch. You know something about that?"

His smile faded. He started to turn his head to look over his shoulder, but I tightened my grip to keep him looking at me.

"I'll take that as a yes," I said. "Because I know this isn't the time or place. But when we get out of here, we're going to have a long talk."

He recovered smoothly, but his smile was thinner as he shrugged and said, "Whatever you say, big sis."

Rolling my eyes, I risked another glance over his

shoulder and saw the man moving away from us now. "Okay, let's go."

I linked my arm with his this time, and within minutes we were cashed out and heading out to the parking lot. I jerked my arm free of his as soon as we exited the building.

"Where to?" he asked.

"That depends. Where are you staying?" I automatically started in the direction of my car. It wasn't snowing at that moment, but it was still cold, so I stuffed my hands in the pockets of my re-donned coat.

"Hotel." He shrugged. "You?"

"Home. I was hoping for something a little more specific."

"So was I."

I was frustrated again, and we hadn't even made it to the car, so I pressed my lips together and said nothing more until we got there. He still hadn't offered any clarification, and when I stopped by the car to look over at him, he was looking around casually like he hadn't a care in the world. It wasn't difficult to imagine how he got himself into this situation.

"So, you're not going to tell me which hotel? I could drive you back. We could talk on the way."

"I'd rather see where you live, if it's around here."

"I'd rather you didn't."

He gasped and pressed a hand over his heart. "You wound me."

"Fuck you," I spat, and this time I was pretty sure the shock on his face was genuine. Unfortunately, so was the confusion. I turned away with a little growl, stalking toward the driver's side door, unlocking it on the way and yanking it open once I got there.

"So, I guess that means I can't drive?" Dan said, but opened the passenger door and slipped inside.

I didn't answer, instead just slamming the door and jamming the key in the ignition.

"Em..." He laid a hand on my arm. There was genuine concern in his voice. It just made me more frustrated.

I brushed his hand off and started the car, letting it warm up while I tucked my hands under my arms and tried to sort through the tangle of thoughts and emotions that seeing him again had provoked.

"God, you're as good at the silent treatment as Mom."

If he wanted to get a rise out of me, he picked the right tactic. I looked over at him, eyes flashing in the late afternoon sun streaming through the frosty windshield. "You don't know anything about me," I began, but again... time and place. "But this isn't about me. This is about you. What the hell are you doing in Santa Fe?"

"Vacationing?" He shrugged. "Heard there was some good skiing out this way."

"Uh-huh. So why aren't you staying at the resort?"

"Keeping my options open. Can we go now?" He glanced in the direction of the casino warily. Maybe he didn't want that guy to come out and find us out here. I studied him in profile for a moment. He looked a lot like Liam, or at least what I remembered Liam looking like. Liam would have been about his age, a few years older, when I left home for good.

"Fasten your seatbelt. The tribal police don't fuck around." I followed my own advice before I backed the car out of the parking space and started maneuvering my way out of the parking lot.

Driving was probably the best thing for me, really. It gave me something to focus on besides the infuriating man sitting beside me. For his part, he did buckle up and sat there quietly until we were moving down the highway toward town. I was careful to set the cruise control to the speed limit on account of the aforementioned tribal police. We hadn't gone more than a mile before we saw one of their fancy sports cars parked on the shoulder, a radar aimed out the window. Really, you'd think the casino netted the tribe enough money without speed-trapping all the tourists on top of it.

We drove several miles in silence. "So, do you know what happened to Christina and Victoria?" I asked eventually.

He nodded, somber, at least for the moment. "Yeah. Tracy told me."

Well, that was surprising news. "Tracy?"

"Yeah, she's another witch from their coven."

I snorted. "I know who Tracy is." I must have snapped a little, because he held up his hands in a placating gesture. "When did she tell you?"

"Uh, well, she called me yesterday to tell me about Tori. As for Christina... I found out about her a week or so ago."

I laughed. "She has your phone number... wow, that's rich."

"What? Why?" He seemed genuinely confused, and it just made me laugh harder.

"Because she was doing a really good job of pretending she was helping Hector look for you."

"Oh, that." Dan smiled, and so help me I wanted to smack him again. "Yeah, she's running a little interference for me. She's been great."

"Please tell me you're not fucking her," I said with a little groan. Okay, so maybe it was blunt of me, but I don't think it was completely out of line.

"Tracy? No. I mean, I probably would if she wanted to. But she's pretty into Hector."

"Okay, you can stop there. So, you do know that Christina's husband wants to kill you, right?" I turned on the blinker to change lanes, passing a slower-moving car.

"Yeah, but that's old news. He got in my face, made some threats. That was weeks ago."

"Weeks ago?" I glanced over at him again, frowning. "How long have you been on vacation?"

He shrugged, scrubbing at his scalp absently with his fingertips. "Haven't been keeping track."

"Don't you have something... I don't know... better to do?"

"Nope."

"Must be nice." We were getting off-topic, so I tried to bring us back to the matter at hand. "Okay, so you know Christina and Tori burned out. Do you know how?"

"No. I didn't assume they were related. Were they?"

I could feel him looking at me, but I kept my eyes on the road. "How am I supposed to know? But Hector sure seems suspicious, and he's convinced Joseph has it in for you, like you were somehow involved."

"Hector's a dick."

"That was my impression too," I murmured, barely aware I'd said it out loud.

He grinned again. "Finally, we agree on something."

CHAPTER 11

Dan didn't have much to go on when it came to what caused Tori and Christina to burn out, but he insisted he had nothing to do with it. More to the point, he didn't understand why anyone would think he had something to do with it. There was little I could do in the end but take his word for it.

I dropped him off at the Hilton downtown and headed back to my apartment. I was way too uneasy about my reunion with Dan to bring him home with me, but we exchanged phone numbers before we parted ways so we could reach each other if need be. I hoped he could manage to stay out of trouble for the rest of his vacation. Also, that it'd be over soon, and he'd go back to wherever it was he usually infested.

It was evening by the time I got home. I'd stopped by a sandwich shop on the way to grab something to eat. I'd skipped lunch, and skipping meals wasn't something I did often or happily. I plugged my phone into my laptop, then kicked off my shoes and settled on the couch for what I was sure would be the best thing I'd put in my mouth hole all day. However, as I was about to bite into a delicious-looking turkey club—to the musical accompaniment of Barrington crunching kibble in the kitchen—my phone buzzed against the coffee table. Leaning over, I peered at the message displayed on the lock screen

Matt: OMW. We're still on, right?

Shit. I'd completely forgotten I was supposed to go out with Matt. What a crazy twenty-four hours it had been.

Me: I'm on it. Eating now. Grab something on the way?

A little margarita therapy sounded like just what the doctor ordered. At least I was still dressed for going out. The phone buzzed again within seconds. That's my Matt, fastest thumbs in the West.

Matt: Ok.

I noticed a few other missed messages, including one from Liam. He'd come through with Dan's number, but I had that taken care of. He also asked me to call him when I had a chance, so I put it on my mental to-do list, right behind, well, everything.

As I reached for my sandwich again, I did some mental math. If Matt was just leaving work, he was about forty-five minutes away with traffic. Pad it with fifteen minutes to stop and grab food, and I had about an hour to kill. I turned on the television while I finished my sandwich, leaning back into the fluffy pillows of my secondhand couch and putting my feet up on the coffee table. It was one of the habits I'd picked up since leaving home. Okay, to be fair, it was one of the habits I'd *cultivated* since leaving home. It was right up there with not making my bed and leaving my clothes wherever the hell I wanted—little acts of rebellion gleefully committed, simply because there was no one around to tell me not to.

The news was on. Someone once told me that they

really ought to call it the "bad news" because that's really all it was. We don't have any big network affiliates in Santa Fe (PBS doesn't really count), so all of the nightly news broadcasts come out of Albuquerque. I did mention it was kind of a small town, right? Anyhow, the stations in Albuquerque do their best to cover the news in Santa Fe too so it's not like we exist in a black hole where nothing happens that well-groomed strangers don't talk into a camera about. Mostly, I wanted to catch the weather, but they just kept teasing it, so I grabbed my laptop once I'd finished eating—I had pretty strict rules about food and my computer since losing one to a terrible soup accident—and was about to check the forecast when I noticed I had new emails waiting. Guess where I clicked? Yeah, I'm easily distracted.

Amidst the usual junk that slipped past the spam filter, I found a message from a friend inviting me to a gallery opening, a plea from a co-worker to cover a shift for her the next day, and a few emails from Matt sent over the course of the afternoon asking, in this order: if I liked my new phone, if I had set up my email yet, when I would get around to setting up my email, and if I wanted him to set up my email for me. Laughing, I fired off a quick reply.

Me: Yes, no, eventually, and only if you want it done quickly. Respectively. -Em

I was still snickering when my phone vibrated again. Answering it was a logistical challenge due to it being on the coffee table with my feet while my laptop was on my lap. Fortunately, I managed to catch it before it went to voicemail. It was an unknown number, so I figured it was a telemarketer.

"Em's house of pain, will it be whips or chains?" I chirped, giving in for a moment to my inner thirteen-year-old.

"Miss Davenport?" The voice had a vague ring of familiarity to it, but I couldn't place it. Female, a hint of nasal but not too unpleasantly so.

"Speaking."

"Oh, good. This is Suzi. Um. Russell's wife?" There was hesitation in her voice, uncertainty. Not that she wasn't sure if she was who she claimed, more that she wasn't sure if I was connecting the dots properly. For once, I was. I'd met Dr. Carson's wife at the office Christmas party last year—a tall woman with long dark hair, endless legs, and at least a hint of Asian in her blood. I wanted to hate her for being prettier than I was, but she was actually really nice too. Damn her.

"Oh! Hey, Suzi, is everything okay?" I wasn't even sure how she got my number. Did Russell have it? I couldn't remember giving it to him, but...

"Yes," she said quickly, then seemed to reconsider. "Er, no. I mean, it's fine now."

I frowned, not sure where this was going. "You've got my attention. What's up?"

"I keep dreaming of you. I think it's important. There's a dark shadow covering half of your face, and a man with silver hair and lightning in his eyes."

I confess, that's not where I thought she might be going with the whole "I dream of you" thing. Hey, I've gotten stranger phone calls. "Okay..."

"Maybe it's just my subconscious at work, but I thought I should let you know. Sometimes dreams, they work in ways we don't understand. Be careful. I think... I think something dark is coming." She paused, then added, "Or someone."

Precognition is totally a thing. I mean, I haven't experienced it myself, but I've heard that it's among the gifts that witches can sometimes possess. Everyone's magic is different. The only thing that made me skeptical was that Suzi wasn't a witch. I would have noticed when I met her. And *then* maybe I could have hated her. I'm not saying I hated witches. I'm just saying that I didn't particularly want anything to do with them—which was making my current position with Dan and Hector's coven such a pain in the ass.

Then again, I wasn't a witch either, and I could sense magic. Men in glass houses shouldn't throw stones and all that.

"Wild," I answered, after perhaps too lengthy of a pause. "Well, thanks for letting me know. I appreciate it." A knock on the door saved me from trying to figure out what else to say. "I've got to go, there's someone at the door. Thanks again, Suzi."

I hung up without waiting for an answer, hopping to my feet and heading to the door with phone in hand to let Matt in.

"Since when do you—" I blinked, finishing after a beat. "Knock?"

The man from the casino was standing on my doorstep.

CHAPTER 12

He seemed as surprised to see me as I was to see him. That was a point in his favor. It meant he hadn't come looking for me specifically. But if he wasn't looking for me, why was he here?

It's funny how many things can flash through your mind in situations like this. No more than a few seconds could possibly have passed, but in that time I considered shutting the door in his face and calling the police. I considered going on the offensive, demanding to know who he was and why he was looking for Dan. I considered just playing dumb. Who, me? No, I wasn't at the casino. It must have been my doppelgänger. Wearing this exact outfit. Crap.

"Hi, um, can I help you?" is what I ended up saying, figuring that playing dumb wasn't really going to get me anywhere. Plus, there was always the chance he'd just happened to move in next door. Okay, maybe not.

He recovered from his surprise quickly, flashing a smile and reaching into his pocket to remove a leather wallet. "Sorry to disturb you at dinnertime, ma'am, but I have a few questions for you if you don't mind. Detective Mike Escobar,

Santa Fe PD." He flipped open the wallet, showing off his shiny metal badge.

Mike. Not Joseph. And a cop? I was so screwed, but I tried to play it cool, giving him the closest approximation to a confused look that I could muster on demand. "Is something wrong? Was there a noise complaint or something? I was just watching the news." The television was still on in the living room, so at least I had something resembling an alibi to back me up there.

"No noise complaint, no ma'am." He shook his head as he tucked his badge away again. "May I come in? You're letting your heat out."

I was, and given that the heat was actually working again, I didn't want to tax the system more than necessary. Still, there was hesitation in me even as I nodded and stepped aside, holding the door open. "Sure, come on in. Do you want something to drink? I have some soda and orange juice."

He wiped his feet on the mat outside—brownie points for him—and stepped inside, glancing around my sparsely decorated living room in the process. "Water would be great, thank you."

I closed the door and headed for the kitchen. "Have a seat. I'll be right back."

Though I quickly got a glass down from the cupboard, I took my time about getting a bottle of water from the fridge and opening it to fill the glass. Don't drink the tap water here, it's got all sorts of crazy shit in it.

"You have a lovely home," the detective said from the next room.

"Hah. You're too kind," I answered, while my thumbs furiously manipulated the pixelated keyboard on my phone's face, firing off a quick text to Matt.

Me: Cop here. Sooner would better.

I could imagine him blinking and cursing as he read the message off the phone cradled in its dashboard holder. There was no immediate reply; he was probably still driving.

Tucking the phone in my pocket, I walked the glass of water out into the living room. "Hope you like it cold."

"Cold is fine, thanks." He waited for me to sit down and followed suit, settling at the opposite end of the sofa with the middle cushion and my laptop in between us. "You were at the casino earlier today, right?"

I smiled, tucking a lock of blond hair behind my ear. All the curl had probably fallen out of it by now; my hair was iron straight and tended to revert to its natural state quickly.

"Yeah. It's my day off." I didn't know what else to say. I was looking for someone? It didn't seem like lying was a great idea at this point.

Escobar sipped the water before leaning over to set the glass on the coffee table. I knew what he was reaching for when he slipped his hand into his jacket, and he didn't disappoint. The photograph came out, and he held it out to me. "See anyone you recognize?" he asked.

I took the picture from him and glanced at it, even though I didn't really need to. "Yeah."

"So, you know why I'm here?" he prompted, leaning back again and draping an arm along the back of the couch. On the whole, he looked too damn comfortable on my damn couch.

"Not exactly," I answered, still sticking with the truth. Mostly. "But I'm guessing this is about Tori?"

He nodded, and I didn't have to look up to know his brown cop's eyes were watching me. Weighing. Measuring. "How did you know Miss Young?"

"I didn't know her," I said, offering the photo back to him.

He raised a brow and said nothing, waiting for me to continue. He didn't even reach for the photo, just let me hold it out to him.

"Not well, I mean. Not personally. I've seen her around. She's local. Was local." I set the photo down on top of my laptop for now. "Am I in some sort of trouble?"

"Should you be?" he asked. Notice how he kept turning every answer into a question? I did too and frowned.

"Not that I know of." They say you shouldn't fold your arms when you're in a conversation, that your body language makes you look guarded, closed off. I did it anyway. I was both, and I didn't mind showing it.

Escobar smiled, appearing so at ease that I itched to turn the tables somehow. "Well, I guess that's good then."

Barrington hopped up on the couch between us and sniffed at Escobar's pant leg. The detective stroked him absently, and he flopped over onto his side across the man's lap. Traitor.

"I'll cut to the chase, Ms. Davenport. You strike me as the sort of woman that might appreciate that."

I nodded, silently willing my cat to at least start licking himself.

"I know it's difficult for you to trust someone in my position, being someone in your position, but I could really use your help."

My position? "I'm really not sure how I can help."

"I know you called in that tip. Thank you, by the way. It was very helpful. We were able to locate her next of kin in Arizona."

Grimacing, I reached up to rub the side of my neck but gave him a brief nod. "It didn't seem right, knowing and not telling anyone. But I don't really know much more about her."

"But you knew she was an unregistered practitioner?" he probed, fingers rubbing behind Barrington's ears. I could hear the creature purring from the other end of the couch. I'd never seen the cat react so positively to someone. I couldn't decide if it made me trust Escobar more or less.

"Yes," I said, still not sure what he was getting at.

"You're not a registered practitioner either."

So that's what this was about. I couldn't help but laugh, while he looked at me quizzically. Finally, the tables were turned! "That's because I'm not. A practitioner. A witch. Whatever you want to call it." I made a dismissive gesture with one hand.

"Alright," he said, after a moment. "So, if you're not part of the rogue witch club, how did you know she was?"

He had me there, and for a moment I wasn't sure what to say. Staring at him wasn't helping, so I reached for the remote and flicked the television off to give myself something to do. "I think this is when I should probably decline to answer any more questions without an attorney present."

Chuckling, Escobar continued to lavish attention upon my cat, but still in that absent way like he was barely aware he was doing it. "I'm not on a witch hunt here, Ms. Davenport. I'm just trying to find out what happened to Victoria Young. She was a young woman in the prime of her life, and one day she just... laid down and died. No medical explanation. So, there has to be a magical one."

"Technically, there was a medical explanation. Her heart stopped beating."

He ignored my snark, just letting it roll off him like water off a duck's back. Smiling again, he shook his head slightly. "You know what I mean. Throw me a bone here. I know you're holding something back. You called her Tori. That's pretty familiar for someone who didn't know her personally."

I grimaced. Damn, he was good. Even if I'd only called her that because Hector and Tracy had.

"Do you know much about the Magic Crimes division of the SFPD?" he asked, shifting tracks sharply enough that I'm sure I blinked.

"What? No." I didn't have to feign cluelessness.

"Magic Crimes investigates crimes against or perpetrated by witches. I *am* the Magic Crimes division of the SFPD. That's it, just me."

"Really?" If I sounded astonished, I was. As soon as magic being real became public knowledge, the government quickly got on board. Every agency wanted practitioners on their staff. Homeland Security, DEA, INS, FBI, CIA—okay, to be fair, the CIA probably had witch agents all along and were glad everyone else was finally getting on board. Santa Fe was a small city, but for a metropolitan area with some eighty thousand residents to only have one detective in their Magic Crimes unit—and a mundie, at that—felt odd. "But you're…"

He smiled wryly. "Not a witch. I used to have a partner, a magical consultant, but about three weeks ago she ate her own gun. Without her, I'm flying blind here. I get the feeling you can help me, or you know someone who can. What do I have to do to earn your trust?"

That was a good question. I don't trust easily, and the way this conversation was going was not helping matters. Escobar's hand stilled, resting atop Barrington's side. The cat didn't seem to like that, shifting and rolling, trying to get his head back under that hand.

"Did you roll in some catnip on the way over here?"

He laughed, shaking his head and giving Barrington's fur a backward ruffle. That was all it took. The cat hopped up and shook himself, then disappeared under the coffee table to start licking his fur back down. Lord Barrington was particular about his coiffure.

"I'm good with animals. I was K-9 before this opportunity came along."

"Why'd you take the job?" I asked, with caution. "It couldn't have made you very popular with anyone."

This time it was Escobar that was rescued by the door, but this time it wasn't a knock. The door simply opened and Matt came inside with a take-out bag in one hand and an all too carefully surprised look on his face. "Oh, hey! I didn't know you had company."

It was all I could do to keep from snickering. The gust of cold air from outside was all it took for Barrington to disappear under the couch.

I didn't bother getting up, just smiled over at Matt. "It's okay, hon. This is Detective Escobar. Detective, Matt."

Matt closed the door and crossed the room with long strides, offering a handshake to Escobar who stood and accepted it. I watched the two men size each other up over the handshake with amusement.

"We were talking about that Jane Doe thing I told you about. The detective was just about to tell me why he became a magic cop."

"A magic cop? That sounds... enchanting," Matt said, with a grin.

I groaned while Escobar chuckled politely. Like he'd never heard that one before, right?

"You really can't help yourself, can you?" I said, rolling my eyes.

"Well, right now I'm going to help myself to a plate. You

two finish up your chat. Ignore me." He squeezed my shoulder in passing, then headed off to rattle around in the kitchen. I heard Barrington meow a moment later and knew he was in there checking out all of the smells.

"You were saying?" I prompted, studying Escobar as he sat down again. The reprieve turned out to be temporary, at best.

"Sorry. I was going to say that it didn't. Make me popular. But I wasn't trying to be popular. I just wanted to do the right thing, to protect *all* the people of Santa Fe, magic-using and otherwise," he answered, with every outward appearance of honesty. I can't read auras or anything, but I believed him.

You'd think that badass spell-slinging witches wouldn't have much to worry about from Joe Normal, but there was a significant spike in violence against witches after they were thrust into the spotlight. Witches are just people and as vulnerable to surprise attacks as anyone else. It didn't take long for hate groups like the Sons of Humanity—basically the KKK without the white sheets and long, sordid history—to start popping up, and they weren't content burning broomsticks on lawns. Witches who used magic to fight back did so at great risk. There are strict laws about how a witch can and cannot use their magic against others, even in self-defense. Technically, I could have pressed charges against Hector for assault, but it would have been his word and Tracy's against mine.

Escobar continued. "So, please. Help me figure out what happened to Tori, so I can give her family some closure and make sure whatever it is isn't still a danger to others."

Another point for him, even if he *was* using interrogation tactics on me. I'd seen my share of procedural police dramas. Use the victim's familiar name to humanize them, right? Even knowing that, he was making it really hard to say no, especially given that I knew what happened to Tori might not be an isolated incident. He didn't know about Christina. Yet.

I sighed and rose from the couch to walk over to the window, looking out on the snow-covered city from my semi-scenic perch. I didn't want to get involved. The tussle I'd had with Hector was fresh in my mind, a reminder of just how powerless I was in their world. But Escobar was in the same position, and he'd lost his backup. Maybe I could help in some way.

"I'm not a witch," I said, finally. "But I may be able to help. I have a, well, I guess you could say it's a magic sensitivity. Plus I know people, people who could maybe supply information if they didn't have to worry about being persecuted—or prosecuted—for it."

I turned from the window to the sight of Escobar turned toward me, a look of relief clear on his face, and Matt standing in the kitchen doorway his mouth hanging open. Apparently, I had defied his expectations.

Great. I hate being predictable.

CHAPTER 13

I really didn't want to work on my day off, but that's what I ended up doing the next morning. One of the downsides of working in nursing is that it's not like an office job where you can call in sick and catch up on missed work the next day. The patients aren't going anywhere, and they still need someone to care for them. If the ward is short-staffed, it's that much harder for everyone. I try to be willing to cover for people when they ask because it makes them more willing to cover for me when I need to take a day. Unfortunately, it meant I had been the designated driver the night before, sipping ginger ale while Matt enjoyed the margaritas. I'd left him sleeping it off on the couch this morning. Lucky him, he didn't have to work today.

Escobar had taken the news about Christina well. He was annoyed that I hadn't brought it up sooner, but more determined than ever to find out what had happened to the two witches. I also explained to him that I was positive Tori had burned out before she died, because I could tell she had no magic left in her. Just like Christina. Burnout wasn't so rare that no one ever saw it happen, but for two witches from the same coven to burn out within a week of one another... something was definitely hinky about that. He said he'd do some digging, and I promised to stop by the police station after my shift. Hopefully, I could fit in a shower, a change of clothes, a meeting with Escobar, and a bite to eat before I was due to meet Barry at the bar where his friend's band was performing.

On the whole, it was going to be a long day, and my work week hadn't even technically started yet. Maybe I could slip out a little early if things were slow.

The morning passed fairly uneventfully, at least for the ER. We got steady traffic but no big traumas or major drama. On my lunch break, I spent some quiet time in one of the on-call rooms after consuming a healthy but bland sandwich from a vending machine in the cafeteria. Or, at least I tried. I was drifting on the edge of a midday snooze when I heard the door open.

"Hey Emily, you awake?" a male voice said, quietly.

Opening my eyes, I turned my head and glanced over at the door. "Yeah, what's up?"

The man the voice belonged to slipped into the room and closed the door, leaning against it. "Sorry to bother you. I know you're on break. I saw you come in here and I thought it'd be a good time to talk."

Now that I had a better view, I could see that it was Russell.

"Talk?" I rolled onto my side, facing him, and curled up some. "About what?" No, I wasn't worried about people thinking we were up to something in the on-call room. That shit only happens on television.

"I hope you're not upset or anything, I looked your number up in the hospital directory for Suzi. She was getting really worked up about those dreams, and I thought it might be good for her to get it off her chest."

Oh right, that. I smiled and shook my head, rubbing my cheek against the pillow in the process. "Well, I guess since you apologized I can cancel that HR complaint."

The color drained from his face, and his eyes went wide, but he processed my smirk a moment later and groaned. "Don't *do* that."

Last year one of the nurses had filed a completely bogus sexual harassment claim against Russell, and it had caused him a major headache. If she hadn't recanted, it would have ended up in his permanent file, and he would have had to deal with disciplinary action. In retrospect, it was mean of me to tease him like that.

"Sorry." I pushed myself up to sit and swung my legs over the edge of the bed. Yawning and leaning back on my hands, I looked up at him with an apologetic smile. "I was just teasing. It's fine. Does she have those sorts of dreams often?"

He gave me a chiding look for my little jab at his expense, then relaxed against the wall. Folding his arms across his chest, he shrugged. "I wouldn't say often, but... fairly regularly, I guess. As long as I've known her. I don't know if it's just her imagination or something more. A few years ago I was heavily leaning toward the former, you know? Now..."

"All bets are off," I finished for him, smiling gently. "I don't know, honestly. You had her checked out, medically?"

He nodded. "Yeah, just to be safe. She's fine, she's just, I dunno. Suzi." But he smiled, and I knew that it was just one of those things he accepted about her because he loved her. Men like Russell gave me hope for the rest of humanity.

"I'll let you know if anything comes of it."

"Thanks." He turned toward the door, then stopped and turned back. "Actually, I've been wanting to ask you about something else. The other day, when that witch went crazy... How did you know?"

I bit my lip, floundering for a reasonable explanation. "He was levitating, Russ. You saw it the same as I did."

"Not when you started chasing us out. I've played it over and over in my mind, trying to figure out what I missed. It was like you saw something we didn't."

My heartbeat kicked up, anxiety flooding my veins as I tried and failed to come up with a good excuse. I liked my job. No, I loved my job. But there was a reason I kept my co-workers in the dark about my background. I didn't want them to look at me differently. I liked being Emily the nurse, judged for my skills and attitude rather than who I shared DNA with.

A knock on the door saved me from having to answer.

A muffled voice asked from the other side, "Emily? Are you still in there? There's a police detective here looking for you."

Russell shot me a quizzical look. Usually, he was the one getting pulled out of conversations, though in his case it was for medical purposes rather than law enforcement ones. So far, anyway.

I just shrugged and gave him a long-suffering smile. "Sucks to be popular, doesn't it?"

∼

IT TURNS OUT, it didn't take an act of Congress to get me out of work that afternoon. All it took was an act of Escobar. While I stood leaning against the wall at the other end of the hall, trying but failing to eavesdrop, the detective had a brief but serious conversation with my supervisor. Whatever he said, she didn't look happy about it, but she nodded and waved a hand at me before walking off in the other direction.

"So, what would've happened if she'd said no?" I asked as he joined me at the end of the hall.

"Well, I do have handcuffs," he said, a little too deadpan.

I laughed. "Man, I'm almost tempted to ask you to do it anyway. It'd give the whole hospital something to talk about for weeks."

He let me change clothes, at least, before whisking me off to his generic sedan. I had barely settled in the passenger seat when he threw the transmission into reverse and backed smoothly out of the parking space.

"So, do I get to know where we're going?" I asked, glancing over at him while I gave the seatbelt a tug to adjust it.

"Crime scene," he said. "We've got another dead witch on our hands. I'm not sure if it's connected..."

"But it's been that kind of week?" I probably shouldn't make it a habit of trying to complete peoples' sentences.

Chuckling, he nodded. "Yeah, exactly. At least this time he was a registered practitioner. I don't know if it's the same coven or not. Maybe you can confirm that when we get there."

"Do you have a name?" I turned my attention out the passenger window as we accelerated into traffic.

"Do you know them all by name?"

"Touché."

The rest of the ride passed in silence, and it was blessedly brief. Escobar was an aggressive—or maybe I should say assertive—driver. He didn't speed, much, but he took corners a little fast and followed the car in front of him too closely for my taste. When he parked the car outside a nondescript house in a residential neighborhood on the east side of town, I pried my fingers off the "oh shit" bar and briefly inspected it for indentations I was sure my fingers had made. If he noticed, he didn't comment.

There were no fewer than three police cruisers, an ambulance, and a fire truck parked outside the house, which wasn't quite the sum total of the emergency response team in Santa Fe but it was not an insignificant number.

"What happened here?" I asked as I joined Escobar on the other side of the car. He was fishing in his coat pockets for something, eventually producing a laminated consultant badge attached to a lanyard that would clue everyone in that I was allowed to be there. I put it on obediently, trying not to think of it as a collar. Heel, Em.

"That's what we're here to find out." He held up the crime scene tape that had been strung up at the edge of the lawn for me to pass under it.

Tabling the rest of my questions for now, I accompanied him across the snow-covered lawn in the direction of the front of the house. A few short steps led up to a wide but shallow porch lined with terra-cotta pots bearing flowering plants in open defiance of the wintry weather. There was a spiderweb of magic coating the outside of the pots, keeping the soil warm and the air around the pots a good forty degrees warmer than everywhere else. One day, someone's going to figure out a way to monetize that sort of thing and make millions, but spells like that don't last without regular maintenance. At any rate, it was clear that a witch lived here. One that specialized in earth magic, specifically.

This impression didn't change as we stepped into the house, which was warm enough that it was practically a sauna. There was greenery everywhere, decorating the living room in various shades of green interspersed with vibrant blooms. There were vines literally climbing the walls. It didn't faze Escobar. He glanced around on his way through the living room, obviously expecting me to follow him. I did.

I could hear conversation elsewhere in the house from the moment I walked in. The kitchen turned out to be the epicenter of the activity. There was a body on the floor, a bunch of those numbered evidence tags littered around the room, and a handful of people at work processing the crime scene. There was also a nasty smell in the room, but it wasn't one I'm entirely unfamiliar with in my line of work. Death isn't pretty, and from the glance I took at the body, it looked like it'd been there a few days.

"Looks like the cavalry is here," someone said, and those present chuckled.

Well, everyone other than me and Escobar, anyway. "What do you have for me, Anderson?" he asked, simply.

A tall, thin man with a shaved head and a chip on his shoulder detached from the wall and approached us, eyeing me. I stared back without comment. Dismissing me for now, he shifted his attention to Escobar. "Bringing your girlfriend to crime scenes now, Esco? That's new."

To his credit, Escobar didn't rise to the bait. "She's consulting," he said simply and waited for the other man to get on with it.

Smirking, Anderson lifted a tablet in his hand and started to read off the pertinent information. "The deceased's name is William Hines. He works for J&L Paper Products. His boss called in a missing person when he didn't come into work for three days. Unmarried, no known relatives. But he's registered, so we called you. Patrol officer found him face down on the kitchen floor." He motioned at the body with one hand. "Obviously dead for several days. Paramedics called, per procedure, to confirm. Body's awaiting your release for transfer to the morgue. No signs of a struggle or forced entry."

"Alright, I'll take it from here," Escobar said, and the other cop presented the tablet to him for a finger signature. Bureaucracy in action. Within minutes, everyone but the crime scene techs had cleared out. I heard the sound of car engines rumbling to life outside moments later. I kind of wished I was in one of them. The novelty of getting out of work to be whisked away on official police business was wearing off fast.

"Emily?" Escobar's voice pulled me back to the here and now. He was holding a pair of latex gloves out to me, and I took them, slipping them on with the ease of familiarity.

"What do you want me to do?" I asked, which earned me a curious glance from one of the lingering techs. Some consultant I was turning out to be.

"Just look around. See if you sense anything or notice anything that seems odd or out of place. Can you tell if he burned out?" He motioned at the corpse, but I shook my head.

"No, not when he's already dead. Sorry."

"It's okay." He started to move carefully around the room. I stayed where I was, not wanting to contaminate anything and wondering if I should be wearing a pair of those little booties on my shoes or something. But I did as instructed, looking around the room for active spells. Unfortunately, I didn't find anything that wasn't obviously related to the plants in some way. It was possible for something to have been hidden amongst those, but I didn't have a clue what I was looking for. Just because I could see spells didn't mean I could necessarily understand them.

We spent about an hour at the crime scene, then headed to the police station.

"Now what?" I asked, settled in Escobar's cubicle in the squad room. There was enough of a mess littering the desk and walls that I couldn't help but feel a sort of newfound kinship with the detective.

Escobar settled behind the desk and set to clearing a space amongst all the unfinished paperwork where we could work, then dropped the case files onto the desktop, where they landed with a solid thud. "Now we look for something that ties the victims together. Can you find out if Hines was in the coven?"

Finally, something I could do. Nodding, I whipped out my shiny new phone and dialed Hector. He picked up on the first ring.

"Hello, Emily." He sounded annoyed, probably because I hadn't been in touch for two days.

"Don't rush excellence," I said, heading him off at the pass. "I need to know if William Hines is a member of the coven."

"I don't know anyone by that name."

"He could go by Bill, Billy, Will? Apparently some kind of earth specialist. Flowering plants on his porch in the middle of winter."

"No, sorry. Have you had any luck locating Dan?"

"I'll be in touch." It wasn't the answer he was hoping for. Hell, it wasn't even an answer, really. But it was the best I could do at the moment. I hung up on him before he could object further, momentarily pleased with myself. The best way to deal with aggressive witches was, apparently, on the phone. *Can't reach me, tentacle boy. Neener, neener.*

Tucking my phone away again, I gave Escobar the bad news. Or was it good news? Either Hines' death was unrelated to the others, or whatever was going on wasn't restricted to Christina and Tori's coven. Either way, it was bad for Hines. Or maybe it just couldn't get any worse.

We spent the next four hours poring over everything in the case files, looking for correlations between the three witches or any indication that they'd had contact with one another. We knew Tori and Christina knew each other, but they didn't seem to intersect with Hines at all. They lived in different parts of town, weren't even close to the same age, and as far as we knew didn't run in the same circles. Then again, we didn't have much information on Hines yet, so we hit a brick wall there quickly.

"Okay, I can't look at any more, the pages are swimming," I declared eventually, closing the file folder I'd been sifting through and pushing it aside.

Escobar looked up from his own and chuckled, reaching for his coffee. I'm pretty sure it was his fourth or fifth cup since we got back to the station. How he wasn't bouncing off the walls, I'd never know. "Take a break," he suggested. "Or, better yet, get out of here. We should have more on Hines by morning."

"Morning? I work tomorrow."

"No, you don't." His eyes lowered to the page again while he sipped his coffee.

"I don't?"

"Nope. Your shift supervisor was surprisingly accommodating."

I'd never known Steel Wool Wendy—so called because she could be about that abrasive—to be accommodating in any sense, so "surprisingly" was the only part of that statement that made any sense. "Okay..." I said, standing to gather up my coat and slip it on. "So, when *do* I have to work again?"

"When we're finished," he said, all too casually.

"Am I getting paid for any of this time off?" I narrowed my eyes suspiciously.

He glanced up again and flashed an apologetic smile. "Sorry, I'm not a miracle worker. But I can probably get you a consulting fee from the SFPD."

"Probably? Well, it'd better keep Barrington in kibble or I'm *probably* dropping him off at your place."

Escobar laughed, a deep rich laugh that resonated even in the busy noisy squad room. "I'll buy him some myself if I have to."

Great. Well, at least one of us would eat.

CHAPTER 14

It was a good thing Escobar let me go when he did because it turns out I had just enough time to run home, feed the cat, scarf a sandwich, and get ready for my second date with Barry. It just figured that my normally quiet life would get shaken up right when I found a nice guy to go out with.

I met him at a dive bar on the outskirts of town, where I discovered that his roommate was in an all-witch band. To my surprise and joy, they didn't use their magic to cover up bad musicianship and were actually great. I enjoyed the outing quite a bit, though I had to turn my phone off early on when Dan—apparently bored out of his gourd—started blowing it up with a barrage of attention-seeking text messages.

I didn't turn my phone back on again until I was settled in the car at the end of the night, giving it a chance to warm up. I had almost two dozen new text messages from Dan, but he'd finally given up about an hour ago. It was late, but I decided to call him back anyway in the hope that I'd wake him up.

He answered on the first ring like he'd been sitting there holding his phone. Waiting. "Hey, sis! What's going on?"

"Jackass. I have better things to do than babysit you on a Friday night, you know."

"That, dear sister, is extremely debatable. Besides, I don't need a sitter. I need a comrade—a mischievous marauder after my own heart!"

"Then why the hell are you bothering *me*?" I asked, latching the phone into its cradle before starting to back my car out from between its neighbors.

"Whoa, whoa, no need to get testy. Damn. You need to loosen up. When was the last time you got some action?"

Longer than I'd care to admit. But that wasn't why I was gritting my teeth and holding the steering wheel in a death grip. "Daniel," I said, in a calm voice that in no way conveyed my annoyance. "What do you want?"

He sighed, audibly. "I thought that was pretty clear. I'm bored. Want to do something?"

"It's 11 p.m."

"So? Tomorrow's Saturday, right? You don't have to work." I doubted he was psychic, so he must have been assuming.

He was right, though, I didn't have to work—not at the hospital anyway. But that was beside the point. "You can't just waltz into my life after ten years and just... be you."

"I'll be whoever you want if you'll bring me a pizza."

"Daniel?"

"Emily?"

"Get bent."

"That's the spirit!"

Don't drive angry, don't drive angry. "I'm not coming over. I'm going home."

"Ohhh. Did you have a hot date?"

"None of your business."

"You did have a hot date!" He was worse than Matt, I swear.

"I'm hanging up now."

"Wait, wait, wait, there's something important I need to talk to you about."

I let my finger hover over the disconnect button. "So help me, if this is about a pizza..."

"Oh my god, would you stop talking about food? I'm starving. But seriously, I think I know what happened to Tori and Christina."

Was he really that desperate for some entertainment, or was he actually serious? "I'm listening."

"A homunculus."

"Remind me what that is?"

"A magical construct, created to do its owner's bidding."

"Oh, right." I was pretty sure I'd never heard of such a thing, but he undoubtedly had way more schooling in the arcane than I did.

"If you don't refresh the spells that animate it, it falls apart. But the longer it remains alive, the smarter it gets."

"Okay. So, you think someone is using a homunculus to make witches to draw too much power?"

"Not exactly. I think maybe someone who had an old homunculus died or lost control of it, and that homunculus is basically 'eating' magic to sustain itself." He sounded... excited. Which was more than a little creepy, given the circumstances.

"Why do you sound happy about that?"

"Because it's super cool."

"People are *dying*."

"Not that," he replied, in something closely resembling a

whine. "Another possibility would be a magic-devouring creature, which is much more boring."

"Are there many of those?"

"In folklore? Sure, throw a rock and you'll hit one. Do they actually exist? Who knows."

He'd actually given me some decent information. Maybe that's why I decided to tell him about my work with Escobar. By the time I was finished filling him in on everything I'd learned—which, granted, wasn't a ton—I was almost home. He didn't interrupt or make a single wisecrack. Maybe he'd dozed off. It had been a while since he said anything.

"You still there?" I asked, because it never hurts to check.

"I want to help."

That was unexpected. "I don't really see how that's possible, I mean, you're still a person of interest. Escobar is still looking for you."

"So, tell him I'm not involved. Be my alibi."

"I can't just be your alibi, that's not how it works. I have to actually have been with you when one of the witches burned out."

There was a long pause, and then he offered, "I don't suppose it helps that the night Christina burned out, I was with Tori?"

Rolling my eyes, I smirked mightily but there was no one else in the car to see it. "No, that doesn't help. I think it's best if you lay low for now."

He sighed. "Fine. But just because I'm laying low doesn't mean you can't call. Use me."

"Daniel..."

"Use me. Please." He was practically pleading, and I had to admit that what I'd told Hector was true. Dan did know what he was talking about when it came to magic, and he very well could be useful with the investigation. So long as Escobar didn't arrest him. Then again, maybe even then.

I sighed, turning on my blinker and pulling into the parking lot outside my apartment. "Fine. But all of this information is need-to-know. Don't go blabbing it to anyone. Seriously. I could get in major trouble, I signed a Non-Disclosure Agreement." A little white lie never hurt anyone, right? Then again, why hadn't I had to sign an NDA?

"Cross my heart."

I was willing to wager—for now—that he still had one.

CHAPTER 15

I showed up at the police station the next morning with donuts. I wasn't sure if it would go over well or they'd all be mildly offended. I mean, cops plus donuts is a big stereotype, but I'd wanted to stop and get coffee on the way in, and you know how it is. One thing leads to another, and the next thing you know you've got a dozen donuts in a variety of mouth-watering flavors. What, that's never happened to you?

Anyway, the temp badge Escobar had given me the day before was good enough for the desk sergeant, who waved me back without any particular fanfare. I found my way to Escobar's cubicle in the squad room, rounding the corner with box in hand.

"I didn't know what you..." I began, trailing off as I saw Escobar wasn't alone. There was a witch sitting across from him in the chair I suspected still had my ass-print in it after yesterday's sit-a-thon. He wore black pants and a dark gray button-up shirt with a patch of some sort on his left sleeve. It wasn't until he twisted in his chair to look at me that I noticed the black tie, badge, and little silver nameplate reading PAYNE.

"Ah, there she is. Emily, this is Deputy Payne from the county Sheriff's Office. Deputy, this is my new consultant, Emily Davenport."

The deputy raised a brow. "Davenport, eh?" He eyed me with cool brown eyes. His cheeks were pitted and borderline gaunt, his skin dark as a walnut. Long black hair was gathered back in a low ponytail. He didn't get up.

"Nice to meet you," I said, automatically. "Donut?" I flipped the box open, displaying it to the two men before setting it on the desk. They didn't resume their conversation, but they did both pick out donuts. There wasn't enough empirical evidence to proclaim it a "cop thing" yet. I mean, who doesn't like donuts? The gluten-intolerant aside. "Do you want me to step out so you can talk? I can take a walk," I offered, still holding on to my coffee cup. I hadn't brought enough of that to share.

"No, it's fine. You should be here for this anyway." It took a moment for Escobar to realize why I was still standing, at which point he hastened to his feet and ducked out of the cubicle long enough to rustle up something for me to sit on.

"Thanks." I hung my coat on the back of the chair and plopped down. "So, what's up?" As I spoke, I leaned forward to snag the corner of the donut box and picked one out for myself. Raspberry jelly-filled? Yes, please.

Of course, the flaw in that plan was that it's all but impossible to eat a jelly-filled donut with anything resembling decorum. You end up with sugar all over your lips and fingers, and usually dribbles of jelly along with a generous dusting of sugar on your shirt. Or, at least I usually do. I did the best I could under the circumstances, cupping a napkin under it to keep from making a total mess. I like to think you can tell a lot about a person by the kind of donuts they like, sort of like you can tell a lot by their shoes. Escobar picked a chocolate iced one with chopped nuts on top, while Payne went for a blueberry cake donut. Anyone that goes for the cake donuts has a traditional streak. Mark my words.

"I called in Deputy Payne for a consult," Escobar said, which came as a surprise. You know, because he had come to me with hat in hand, all but begging me to consult because he had no alternatives. While I was having a brief but rapid internal debate about whether or not to bring this up, Escobar settled his eyes on the Native American man across the desk and took a sip of coffee to wash a mouthful of donut down before finishing his thought. "Three weeks ago."

Now I was a whole other level of confused, given that it had only been a few days since Tori burned out. A different case, maybe?

Payne just smirked. "It's a big county, detective. There are many that have need of my services. I have to prioritize as best I can. There was no indication that Ms. Gentry's death was anything but the tragic actions of a deeply troubled woman."

The way he said "prioritize" sounded suspicious, but I did my best to keep my expression neutral and my mouth shut—which wasn't hard since it was full of gooey raspberry donut. Mention of Ms. Gentry—who I assumed was Escobar's previous consultant—did pique my interest, though. I glanced between the men, picking up a hint of something from Escobar, but I couldn't put my finger on it.

Escobar was not impressed, that much I could tell, but he didn't seem inclined to pick a fight about it. He just leaned back in his chair with a donut in one hand and his coffee mug in the other. "Right. Well, as I was saying, we may have a bigger problem on our hands now, so it's a good thing you're here."

Payne just smirked, polishing off his donut in no more than three bites and reaching for another one. "I'm not aware of any burnouts elsewhere in the county, but they're not the sort of thing that generally gets reported to the police unless a death is involved. Even then, traditional Navajo are so touchy about burial that they've usually got their dead in the ground before they call in a report."

He wasn't kidding. I'd heard that some of these very traditional Indians believed that even touching the dead person's body would keep their spirit tied to the Earth. Sometimes they went so far as to punch a hole in the wall of the person's house to allow their spirit to escape. Burial was swift, usually before the next sunrise, and the graves were left unmarked. It was even considered bad luck to speak the name of the deceased, possibly causing their spirit to return to torture the living.

"Yeah, I know," Escobar said, a hint of annoyance creeping into his tone. I was starting to think these two had history.

Payne just kept smirking and wolfed down donut number two.

"Do we have a time of death on Hines yet?" I asked, in an effort to distract them both. Hines. Look at me, day two and I was already picking up the habit of calling people by their last name.

"Sort of." Escobar reached for his notepad. "Best estimate is four days ago."

I considered where that fell in the timeline with the others. "Do you have a calendar?" Doing all the math in my head was not working very well.

Escobar reached behind him to unpin a calendar from

his wall and offered it to me. I set the remains of my donut on a napkin and wiped my fingers, then grabbed a pen from the cup on Escobar's desk and started making some notes. "Okay. Tori died on the sixth, technically. But she burned out on the fifth." I remembered it because it had been my birthday when she was brought into the hospital. "That was four days ago, the same day Hines died. We don't know if he burned out first, but if he did it couldn't have been more than a day or two before that because his boss said he'd only missed three days of work, right?"

"Right," Escobar said, leaning forward in his chair and sipping his coffee, clearly interested to see where I was going with this. Deputy Payne just sat there watching, indifferent as far as I could tell.

"Christina burned out... I don't have an exact date, but it was about a week—minus a day or two—before Tori." I marked that on the calendar too and then looked up at Escobar. "When did your partner die?"

"November sixteenth," he answered, precisely enough that my eyes lingered on him a moment. "You don't think her death was related, do you?" He didn't sound like he liked that notion much. I couldn't blame him.

"I wouldn't rule it out, though I'm not sure a burned-out witch would be capable of self-harm. Did she have a history of depression?"

"Not that I know of."

Payne interjected, "It *is* the silent killer."

"Actually, that's high blood pressure." I eyed Payne a moment, then went back to the calendar. I was hoping to see some sort of a pattern, but it wasn't materializing. Unless... "It needs more to sustain it."

I looked up to find both men staring at me. Setting down the pen, I reached for my coffee again. "One of the theories

I'm working on. A homunculus." Okay, technically it was Dan's theory but I couldn't tell them that on account of him being a person of interest I was harboring.

Payne snorted. "A magical construct is sustained by its creator," he said with all the arrogance of a man who thinks he knows everything.

"Yeah, but what happens when its creator dies? Or burns out? It loses that tether."

"Then it dies."

"Right, but it doesn't happen immediately, does it? It has some magic left to run on. What if it figures out how to sustain itself by siphoning magic from other witches?"

Payne folded his arms. "They're not that smart."

"The older they are, the smarter they get." It wasn't even my theory, but I resented the way he wanted to dismiss it out of hand. Meanwhile, Escobar's eyes bounced between us as if he were watching a fascinating tennis match while he finished his donut.

Payne sat there frowning for a few moments more, then shrugged. "I suppose it's plausible, but I don't know how likely it is."

I set my coffee down and reached for the remains of my donut. "But *if* it's possible, the longer the homunculus persists, the more magic it might need, which would account for escalation. Hell, it could have been doing this for a long time, but it didn't need so much that it was in danger of burning anyone out until now."

Escobar finally spoke up, glancing between Payne and me. "Okay, well, that's one thought. But if it is a homunwhatas... how do we track it?"

"Homunculus." I studied my donut for an uncomfortable moment, then shrugged. "I have no idea." I bit off as much donut as I could chew, to give myself a chance to think.

Payne licked his fingers, then wiped them on his uniform pants and dusted crumbs from his chest. "Not my problem," he said, earning a frown from me. It didn't seem to bother him any. "I suggest you try some old-fashioned police work and see if you can find anything that would link the victims. If they are, indeed, victims of something besides their own hubris. You do know that ninety-nine percent of all burnouts are accidental, entirely the fault of the witch, right?"

"Yeah, I know," I said. "But you know it doesn't happen this frequently either. Two or three in a week, in a town this size? Maybe in Los Angeles or New York, but Santa Fe? There just aren't enough witches by sheer population density."

Ignoring me, he addressed Escobar. Zero points for him. "I'll be in town a few more hours. Call me if there's something you need me to look at."

With that said, Deputy Payne exited the cubicle and disappeared around the corner.

I must have given Escobar a questioning look because he shrugged. "He's the only witch on the county sheriff's payroll, so he's stretched pretty thin. He's right, though. We have some good old-fashioned police work to do."

I popped the last bite of donut in my mouth and resisted the urge to reach for another one. It was going to be a long day.

CHAPTER 16

Escobar and I worked through the day poring over case files, evidence, and rap sheets for the "usual suspects" looking for any links between or to the victims. The lunch hour came and went without either of us noticing.

By the time I left the station, I was starving. I checked my phone while I considered what to pick up on the way home for dinner. It'd buzzed a few times over the course of the day, but I'd ignored it. I had a message from Matt, checking in like any other Saturday, one from Barry, asking if I'd had a good time at the concert, and one from Dan. Just one, rather than a flurry of them.

Dan: want 2 get something 2 eat?

Well, I did. And while I didn't necessarily want to hang out with my annoying, slightly-less-estranged-than-he-had-been-a-few-days-ago brother, I felt like maybe this hint of personal growth ought to be rewarded. Or at least not ignored. The message was less than an hour old, so I fired off a reply and hopped in my car.

We met at my second-favorite restaurant in Santa Fe, Tres Hermanos. Normally I'd be all in for the Tin Whistle, but I didn't want to risk an encounter with Hector. After all, I hadn't held up my end of the bargain. I'd found Dan, but I hadn't filled Hector in on that—or anything else I'd been up to involving his burned-out friends. How much of it was actually his business was debatable, anyway.

The warmth and fragrant aromas washing over me as I stepped inside made my stomach rumble loudly. The place was packed, standing room only in the waiting area with some spillover outside. I found Dan inside, flirting with the hostess.

"There she is!" Dan exclaimed upon seeing me, his lips curved in a broad smile. "I got us on the list already. The lovely Gabrielle here says our table is just about ready." He turned his attention back to the hostess, who was blushing but flowering under his attention. "Gabrielle is such a cool name..."

It was too late to turn around and go back outside, but I'll admit the impulse was there. Instead, I hovered in the vicinity and soaked in the atmosphere. Did I mention the smells? I felt like I was wrapped in a warm, fresh tortilla. Like a human burrito. Cumin, chile, onion, garlic, and peppers... this was my comfort food.

Dan caught my attention a moment later, and we were whisked away to a small table in the middle of the room. Tired, I leaned on the table and stared at the menu without really seeing it. I knew what I wanted, anyway. Remember that burrito Hector was eating at the cafe, smothered in green chile? I wanted that. I mean, not that specific one because that was days ago and who knew if he got it refrigerated in a timely fashion.

Dan snapped his fingers in front of my face. I probably wasn't paying as much attention to him as he wanted. "Hello? You in there?"

I blinked, focusing on him with a frown. "Yeah, sorry. Long day."

"Tell me about it," he said, surprising me with what seemed like genuine interest. "I spent the whole day doing a whole lot of nothing, so... please. Let me live vicariously through you."

"Eh, it wasn't that interesting. I just did some research with Escobar."

"Oh! How's it going? Did you tell him about the homunculus?" he asked, latching onto the topic immediately. I should have expected that.

I flipped the menu closed and sat back in my chair, toying with the edge of the tablecloth while the waitress dropped off our water glasses. As she moved off again to give Dan a little more time with the menu, his attention settled on me once more.

"Yeah, it came up," I said. "I got to meet the witch from the county sheriff's office."

"Was she hot?"

"Why do you assume it was a woman?"

"I didn't, but if it was a guy I don't care if he was hot. Unless you thought he was hot, I suppose. So, was he or she hot?" he asked while studying the menu.

"No, he definitely wasn't hot. He was actually kind of a smarmy asshole. Anyway, we still haven't found anything in particular that would link the attacks—if they even are attacks."

"Have you considered a psychic?"

"Be serious."

"I *am* being serious." He flipped his menu closed and set it aside. Somehow he made slouching in that chair look suave.

"No, I haven't considered a psychic. Even if they pointed

us right to the source, their testimony would be thrown out in court." Prosecuting magical crimes was a tricky business. So much of the evidence is intangible by its very nature, so police still have to rely on more conventional evidence if they want justice to be served. Psychic testimony was the exact opposite of what they needed.

Dan waved a hand dismissively. "Fine, fine. So, this witch. Did he have any ideas?"

"That's the thing." I sighed and rubbed the back of my neck. "He didn't seem particularly interested in helping at all. Like it was just a formality for him to show up for a consult, but he had better things to do. I guess I'm seeing why Escobar wanted my help so badly."

"Why can't he just hire an actual witch?"

"He had one, but she committed suicide a few weeks ago. They haven't hired a new one yet. I don't know what it's like in Boston, but a lot of the witches here don't trust the police."

"And you do?" He sipped his water.

"As a whole, not really. But I trust Escobar." I was glad he didn't ask why, because I wasn't sure I had a good answer for that.

The waitress returned to take our order, and once she left I managed to steer the conversation away from the case and onto other things. Recent movies. Popular music. I had the sudden impulse to get to know Dan better. I quickly discovered that if there's one thing Dan likes to talk about, it's Dan. I didn't mind. I let his chatter wash over me, finding it strangely comforting.

I was about halfway through my delicious burrito when the hair on the back of my neck stood on end. I glanced up from my plate and across the table at my brother. Judging from his expression, he felt it too. A surge of magic. Powerful magic. Sudden, stark, and nearby. I glanced around the dining room, but it wasn't inside the restaurant. If we could feel it, and it wasn't even in the room, that was significant. We didn't say a word, just pushed back our chairs almost simultaneously and grabbed our coats. I think he threw some money down on the table. I'm not really sure, but no one tried to stop us for dining and ditching as we wove our way quickly through the maze of tables to the door.

Even when we got outside, the source was difficult to pinpoint. It wasn't in the immediate vicinity. Outside, people were waiting for tables or milling about the parking lot. We rushed for the sidewalk and looked up and down the street.

"There!" Dan pointed. I turned my head and blinked, seeing a man shining like a star a block away.

We took off running. The power gathered around the man started to shift and roll, twisting into a sinuous rope that rose like a cobra out of one of those snake charmer's baskets. Up and up it went, into the sky. I'd never seen anything like it before, nor the sheer amount of magic coursing through the man. As we got closer, I got a better look at his face. He was older, in his fifties if I had to guess. I got the impression of Hispanic features, but I didn't have time to take it all in. His expression was utterly blank, as if he were in some sort of trance, and the glowing whites of his eyes told me he was nearing his limit, magic-wise.

"Hey! Hello!" Dan snapped his fingers and waved a hand in front of the stranger's face. "Snap out of it, buddy!"

That rope of power continued to snake its way upward, gaining in speed as it arced northwest. The glow around the witch began to dim as it went, but not because he was using less power, more like it was just... leaving.

"Shit, he's gonna burn out! Do something, Dan!"

"What am I supposed to do?" He gave the man's

shoulder a shove to try and shake him out of whatever had gripped him.

"Make him stop! Bind him! There has to be something!"

"I can't!" Dan said, a hint of panic creeping into his voice.

Pushing him out of my way, I reached out and grabbed the man's face between my hands. "You have to listen to me!" I shouted at him, desperate for something, anything, to make it stop. My fingers began to tingle. "STOP!" I cried, knowing full well that this witch was about to burn out right in front of me, and there was nothing I could do to stop it.

Then something happened. The tingling in my fingers spread up my hands, over my wrists and up my arms, until it seemed like my whole body was like one of those dead limbs waking from sleep, phantom pins pricking me everywhere. I screamed, but I didn't let go. I felt his energy flowing into me, filling the space between those pricks with warmth until there was nothing left but warmth and light. The rope of power above us started to reverse its course, returning to the witch it came from... and through him to me. His eyes rolled back in his head, and he slumped to the ground, slipping between my fingers.

With the contact broken, the magic started to drain away. Looking down, I could see it retreating down my fingers and forearms. My eyes were drawn to the ground, which was covered with a spiderweb of mystical energy, stretching outward a good fifteen feet. My feet were at its center.

Dan had retreated to stand at the edge of it as it expanded, having the good sense not to mess with whatever was going on or risk getting caught up in it. "What... the... fuck..." he said with his usual eloquence.

The rest of the power drained out of me, leaving me suddenly cold, the world much dimmer than it had been a moment ago. "I don't— I don't know. *Now* can you bind him?"

"No," Dan said.

I stared at him in confusion. He moved closer, but cautiously.

"Why not? I know he's strong, but..."

"I just can't." His shoulders slumped, and he wouldn't meet my eyes.

A nagging suspicion tugged at the back of my mind, but I was too cold, frustrated, and confused to cope with it right then. I looked around. We'd drawn a few gawkers. Mostly witches, for obvious reasons. Mundies wouldn't have had any clue what was going on.

"Can anyone bind this man? Please, for his own safety," I implored, looking around me. Most just stared or turned around and walked hurriedly away, probably unnerved by what they'd witnessed. It was like those awful things you hear about big cities, where people put their heads down and keep walking rather than help someone being mugged, just... the small metropolis edition. It made me sick. Also, angry.

I thought I was going to have to get down on my knees and beg, but finally, someone stepped forward. A man of obvious Native American ancestry, tall and bronze-skinned with a narrow nose and strong jaw. He strode forward confidently and took a knee beside the fallen man. Stripping off a glove, he lay his hand across the man's forehead. Power flared around him, and I watched as the spell was woven. It didn't take long; he knew what he was doing.

"You should call 911," the stranger said, meeting my eyes. His eyes were like warm, dark pools, drawing me in. "He may have hit his head when he fell."

"Th-thank you," I said.

He smiled, and something inside me twinged.

Behind me, Dan cleared his throat. The moment broken, I glanced over my shoulder at him. "Why don't you make that phone call?" By the time I looked back at the stranger, he was turning to go. "Wait," I called after him. "How can we reach you, to undo the binding?"

We exchanged names and numbers, after which I sat down in the snow to wait for the ambulance while Dan fumbled his way through the 911 call. I suspected he'd never made one before, and trying to give accurate information about your location in an unfamiliar city could be a challenge. As the adrenaline rush slowly faded, my hands started to shake. I tucked them under my arms while I watched Dan, frowning as I mulled over what had happened. And what hadn't happened. Someone had some explaining to do.

Unfortunately, he was probably thinking the same thing about me.

CHAPTER 17

Dan made himself scarce before the cavalry arrived. I suggested we meet up at his hotel, but he'd pressed me until I gave him my address. That would probably come back to bite me, but I was too tired and freaked out to argue with him. Also, I really didn't want Escobar to show up and find him there, even though being present for the attack gave him a strong alibi.

The ambulance arrived first, and I winced as soon as I saw the number on the back of it.

Andy gave me the side-eye but set to work checking out the witch. He was still out cold, which was probably for the best. It was bothersome, though. It's never a good thing when someone loses consciousness. I'd done what I could before they arrived, making sure he was breathing and that no one moved him. It was unlikely he had a neck injury, but if he did, the wrong move could mean permanent paralysis. I certainly didn't want to be held responsible for that.

By the time Escobar arrived, I was sitting on the curb, wrapped in a bright red patient blanket.

"Just can't leave you alone for a moment, can I?" he said as he approached. "What happened?"

Relief flooded me as soon as I laid eyes on him, and I heaved a full-body sigh. Even though there was probably nothing he could do at that point, it was still a comfort having him there. Odd, perhaps, since just a couple of days ago he was a stranger.

After checking to make sure Andy and Michelle were out of earshot, I dove right in. "I was eating dinner down the street and felt a surge of magic. Really powerful magic. I ran outside and found that man"—I motioned toward the ambulance—"gathering a crap ton of magic."

"A crap ton?" He arched a dark brow. "Is that the technical term for it?"

I smirked, feeling like my old self. However temporarily. "Something like that. Anyway, I think we can rule out a homunculus. Whatever happened, it was initiated remotely. There's no way a homunculus could have that kind of finesse. But it was definitely an attack designed to drain magic out of this witch. I've never seen anything like it before. Hell, I've never even heard of anything like it before. It was like someone took his magic, spun it into a rope, and yanked it up into the sky. It was headed kind of that way." I pointed northeast.

Escobar glanced in the direction I motioned. "Okay, so what happened? Did he burn out?"

"No." I looked away.

But he was a detective, so he noticed my hesitation. "What happened?" He sat beside me on the bench.

I was quiet for a long moment, chewing my lower lip, suddenly reluctant to continue. I didn't know what to say about what had happened next, hadn't even begun to process it. "I don't know."

"Did it just stop?"

"No." I sighed and rubbed my temples. "I— I stopped it, but I don't know how. I was trying to shake him out of the trance or whatever it was he was in, because I knew he was in trouble." I looked at Escobar, studying his face by the light of the street lamp. His expression was guarded, difficult to read. "He was going to burn out. I knew it. But when I grabbed him, I just— I don't know. I drained it all away."

Escobar gave me a look that was somewhere between curious and skeptical.

"I'm not lying. That's what happened. Somehow I managed to pull the magic leaving him into me, and ground it like a magic lightning rod. It went into the ground around us, and then he passed out, but... I swear, he's still intact. I don't know what I did, but I stopped it, Mike." The last few words came out in almost a whisper. I'd never used his first name before, much less turned it into a nickname. But right then, for some reason, calling him Escobar just felt too formal. I was baring my soul, in a way. I didn't know what had happened or what it meant. I'd never had any sort of manifestations before, no indications that I was anything but a largely mundane offshoot of a gifted family. A poor facsimile of an actual witch.

He nodded and laid a hand on my shoulder. "Yeah, I get it. That must've been surprising."

I couldn't contain the short laugh that escaped me. "That's putting it mildly. I nearly wet myself."

He laughed too. "That would have been awkward."

"You have a gift for understatement." I chuckled, then breathed a quiet sigh. "Now what?"

"Well, the vic may still be in danger, so we have to figure out how to keep him safe. I think that means keeping him close to you in case the perp tries again."

I grimaced, nodding at first but pausing after a moment. "Well, that's not necessarily true..." Trailing off, I fished out my phone and started dialing.

"What?" Escobar said. "What are you thinking?"

I held up an index finger while I held the phone to my ear with my other hand.

Hector answered on the first ring. "I'm getting a little tired of your games, Davenport."

"Hello to you, too. What are the odds of whoever did those wards for Christina doing some more for me?"

He snorted. "We don't owe you anything."

I rolled my eyes, glancing over at the ambulance. "True. However, you do need something from me and now I need something from you."

"You haven't given me anything."

"I can set up a one-on-one."

"With Daniel?"

"Yes."

He was quiet, thinking about this for a moment. "I'm going to need more information."

"There's a witch in danger. I think whatever happened to Christina happened to him too. If you can help me set up a safe place for him to lay low while we figure this out, I'd really appreciate it." I thought hard about how else I might be able to sweeten the deal, but I didn't have anything else he wanted. I mean, I could have offered him information about my newfound ability, but I wanted to keep that close to the vest. Need-to-know basis.

There was another pause from Hector, but eventually he said, "I'll do it for this witch, not for you. Give me an hour." He gave me an address, and I made frantic gestures at Escobar for a pen and something to write on. He produced both from his coat pocket, like a good Boy Scout.

Afterward, I handed Escobar back his notepad and pen. "Okay, I called in a favor. Sort of. One of the locals is going to—"

"Scare up someone to ward the hell out of something," he finished for me, with a small smile. "I was listening."

CHAPTER 18

It was almost midnight when I finally got home. The witch, Gabriel Sanchez, was safely ensconced within a heavily warded motel room on the SFPD's dime after a brief hospital visit to ensure he was all right. Escobar's boss had wanted to throw him in a cell or interrogation room, but I lobbied against it. He hadn't done anything wrong, and he was even a registered practitioner. Sure, it would have been secure, once warded, but it didn't seem right. To his credit, Escobar backed me up.

I found out that Hector's ward master was the older man I'd sort of met at Christina's trailer. Apparently, he had a particular gift for wards, and he didn't seem to mind using them for Gabriel, even if he made snide comments about me in Spanish to Hector while he did it.

After they left, Escobar had turned to me and asked, "They have no idea you speak Spanish, do they?"

I wasn't sure how he knew either, but he was the professional investigator. For all I knew, he'd been putting together one of those big thick files on me, too.

I didn't see Dan anywhere outside when I pulled into the

parking lot at my apartment complex, but that was probably a good thing. He'd be freezing the family jewels off by now unless he was sitting in a warm car, and I was beginning to suspect he didn't deign to drive himself anywhere. My usual spot was occupied, which was annoying, but I did mention it was almost midnight. When you're out late, you forfeit all parking lot territory when you live with others, social contract or not. I had to park around the back of the building and walk around to the front to get to the stairs since there wasn't a pass-through. By the time I got there, I was yawning and seriously dragging ass, but I made it up the stairs, daydreaming about my warm bed and fluffy pillows. At least, I hoped it was warm. If the heat was out again, I was going to give the building manager a piece of my mind.

When I opened the door, I was greeted by a rush of warm air and a surprising amount of light. Had I left the light on? No. Blinking in the sudden brightness, I quickly discovered why the light was on. Matt was there. No, not just Matt. Matt and Dan, sitting on the couch, munching popcorn and watching a movie. Barrington had assumed kitty meatloaf position on the back of the couch, ignoring them both. And me, for good measure.

"Hey!" They spoke simultaneously and laughed over it. It seemed like they were having a good old time hanging out, which stung. Matt was my friend. I didn't want my brother honing in on my territory. Plus, Dan and I needed to have a long talk. Even if, at that point, I was seriously tempted to put it off until morning.

"Hey." I closed the door and went through the process of shedding my outerwear. While I was at it, Matt must have remembered he was annoyed with me, because he got all frowny and muted the sound on the television.

"I've been trying to reach you all day," he said.

I winced. I couldn't even remember the last time I checked my phone, but I was pretty sure it was before dinner.

"Shit, I'm sorry. Worst friend ever. Is everything okay?" I extracted my phone from my pocket to flip through the messages he'd left me.

"I was wondering the same about you! Fortunately, your brother here assured me you were fine. I found him sitting on the steps like an orphan, practically blue in the face."

Dan made doe eyes at me, all pitiful and shit. My fingers itched to smack him.

"Sorry," I said, apologizing anyway. "I told him it was going to be a while. I had to wait for the ambulance and brief Escobar and…" I trailed off, looking between them. Both men were wide-eyed, but for different reasons. I'm sure Dan was surprised I was "going there" with Matt, while Matt was surprised at the mention of an ambulance. I dropped my face into my hands and rubbed my face. "I'm going to need some coffee."

Matt was more than willing to comply, and since he already had a pot brewed I ended up settled on the couch between him and Dan with my fingers curled around a steaming mug in record time. I filled Matt in on what had happened, then filled them both in on Gabriel being safely tucked away behind magic-stopping wards for the night.

"Well, at least he's safe," Dan said. "For now. But he can't spend the rest of his life in there. That would really suck."

"Yeah. Plus, once the perp figures out he can't get to him, he'll just move on to someone else."

Matt chuckled. "You sound like a cop already."

"I do?" Shaking my head, I leaned forward to set my coffee mug on the table, then shifted to face my brother.

"What did you do?" Okay, so maybe it was an abrupt subject change, and my tone was a little accusatory, but by then it was after midnight and one way or another we had to have it out.

"What do you mean 'what did I do?'" he asked, going on the defensive. It was in the set of his eyes, his posture. Hell, he even cast a furtive glance at the door.

"When we were standing there watching that witch burn out, you should have been able to stop him. Or at least try. But you didn't. You stood there, looking panicked, and said you couldn't. I think I know why, but I want to hear it from you." I kept my gaze level, watching those eyes that were so much like mine. Matt's hand touched my back. I leaned into it, letting a little of the tension that had risen bleed away, and took a slow breath. "Come on, Dan. Talk to me."

I think maybe it was calling him Dan that did it. Usually, I only refer to him as Daniel to his face, a subtle jab for all those years he spent calling me Null. It needled him. He didn't want to be Daniel. It was too stuffy. He was Dan. Relaxed, casual, irresponsible Dan. Danny in a pinch.

He sighed, looking down at his lap. "I can't do magic. I'm under a binding."

No surprises so far. "Uh-huh. Why?"

"Because Mom is pissed at me. She basically disowned me," he confessed, all but squirming in his seat.

That was surprising. My brows went up, but I didn't stop there. "Uh-huh. Why?" I was starting to sound like a broken record, but I was too tired to care.

"I think what she means to say," Matt said, "is that she's sorry to hear that. That sucks."

I shot my best friend a glare over my shoulder. "I can speak for myself, thanks. But yeah, I guess it sucks. Not like I don't know what it feels like." The last was admitted grudgingly as I looked back over at Matt again. "But the question stands. What'd you do to piss her off?"

Dan licked his lips, clearly anxious about the way the conversation was going. "Because a girl I was seeing got pregnant."

I narrowed my eyes, still suspicious there was more to it. "That's it?"

He sighed. "She's a mundie."

Oh. Well, that would explain it. I was quiet for a long moment, mostly because I was trying to stem the tide of hysterical laughter that was bubbling its way up from my insides. I failed, but at least it came out as a snickering chuckle instead of huge guffaws.

Dan looked offended enough as it was, shooting me a glare. "It's not funny, Em! She cut me off! Told me to pack my shit and get out!"

"It's a little funny," I protested, getting myself under control again only to break down in another fit of giggles.

Dan got to his feet, stiffly. He still had his pride, and I felt a little bad for wounding it. A very little.

"Come on, don't be that way." I caught his wrist and tugged gently. "Sit down, let's talk."

He yanked his hand away but sat back down again, this time on the edge of the couch. Leaning forward, he rested his elbows on his legs and put his head in his hands.

Matt nudged me. I both hated and loved that he challenged me to be a better person sometimes. Sighing, I put a hand on Dan's back, giving it an awkward pat. I was a nurse. Comforting people was my job. Yet when it came to my family, I was way out of my element.

"Okay, so... you knocked up a mundie. I can see why she's pissed, why she kicked you out and cut off your allowance. But why did she bind you from doing magic?"

His answer was quiet but audible in the otherwise quiet room. "She said if I liked mundies so much, I could find out what it was like to live like one."

He sounded so miserable, so alone that I couldn't help but sympathize. I'd experienced that isolation, that separation, firsthand. I might not have been able to understand what it was like for someone that grew up with magic to have to live without it, but I knew what it was like to be an outsider in your own family. A pariah. In a way, he was like those burned-out witches except he could still sense the magic inside him. He just couldn't do anything with it.

"That does sound like her," I said, with a grimace. I patted his back some more, then retracted my hand. "So, why'd you come to Santa Fe, of all places?"

"Liam told me you were here. He's been slipping me a little money under the table, but it's not much. I thought maybe you'd understand. Maybe you'd know someone that could undo the binding spell. Maybe you could lend me a little scratch..."

I laughed again, motioning at my humble living room. "Three bare walls and a secondhand sofa. Do I look like I'm rolling in dough? I work for a living. Besides, if you've got enough money to hang out at the casino I don't think you're hurting."

"I don't have much left. I was trying to gamble my way into some more, but you pulled me away before I could get a good streak going. You don't get an allowance?"

I shrugged uncomfortably. "I don't want their money. I haven't accessed that account since I left."

"Christ, Em. In ten years? There has to be like half a million dollars just sitting there gathering interest."

There wasn't. It couldn't have been more than a quarter-million, but it was interesting to find out just how big a gap there was between my allowance and my siblings'. Not surprising, but interesting. At least he didn't ask me to give it to him. Yet.

"So, what are you going to do now?" I asked, changing the subject. I was afraid to look over at Matt, but I knew he was still sitting there being supportive, soaking up all the family drama. At least he hadn't gone so far as to resume eating popcorn.

"Try to get back into her good graces, I guess. Somehow. I thought maybe if I helped you figure out what was going on with the witches here that maybe she'd reconsider, maybe she'd let me at least have my magic back."

I smirked. "That's not what I meant. I meant what are you going to do about the girl you got in the family way?"

"It doesn't matter." He sat back again.

I studied him for a long moment, feeling the corners of my mouth turn downward. I was about to protest that it did matter when he finally turned his head and looked over at me.

"You know," he said, a speculative gleam in his eyes. "I bet Mom'd be interested to find out that her little ugly duckling may be turning into a swan after all."

I narrowed my eyes, frowning again as I eyed him. "Don't even."

He smiled, some of the life coming back into his features. "Don't even what?"

"I'm not going to pay you off to keep your mouth shut."

He widened his eyes, laying a hand over his heart. "Dear sister, you wound me. But now that you mention it, there *is* something you can do for me. Several somethings, actually. Let me help with the investigation, help me find someone to get this binding undone, and let me surf your couch until I get back on my feet."

Anger bubbled inside me. He had some nerve. There he sat, looking all pleased with himself while he held my feet to the fire. And somewhere back east was a young woman he'd abandoned, pregnant and alone.

"My couch has a pull-out," Matt offered.

"No offense, man. You seem like a nice guy but I don't know you. I'd rather stay here."

I drew a deep breath and exhaled slowly, getting to my feet. "Fine. I'll agree to those terms, but not because you might rat me out. I'll do it because you're family. Maybe someday you'll figure out what that means." I turned and walked away, down the hallway to my bedroom where I closed the door with deliberate care not to slam it. I wasn't going to give him the satisfaction of knowing how upset I was, and I wasn't going to let him see me cry.

I crawled into bed fully clothed and curled up around a pillow to do just that. I heard the door open and close quietly after a little while. The light flicked off, and I felt the bed shift as Matt climbed in behind me. He wrapped his arms around me and held me while I cried myself to sleep. One of these days we were going to have to set some firmer boundaries, but this wasn't that day.

CHAPTER 19

The next morning, I woke to the smell of coffee and bacon. I felt like I'd run a marathon. Everything ached, but those fragrant aromas were enough to lure me out of bed. I shuffled down the hallway wearing yesterday's clothes and found Matt in the kitchen making breakfast but my brother nowhere to be found. I didn't miss him.

"My people demand coffee," I mumbled.

He laughed and supplied me with a fresh mug. I leaned against the counter to sip while he served up a couple of plates. French toast, eggs and bacon. He'll make someone a great wife one day.

I wasn't fully awake, but it wasn't hard to notice that there were only two plates and nothing left over for a third. "Where's Dan?" I asked, trailing him out of the kitchen to the table and settling in front of the plate he set down for me.

"Not sure. He was gone when I got up." He set his own plate down and slipped into a chair. Everything we could possibly want was already on the table. "I figured he didn't deserve breakfast anyway."

I snorted, nodding as I set my mug down on the table and reached for the syrup. "Preach it, sister."

The French toast got a light drizzle in the thick, sugary liquid, but after a moment I went ahead and gave the bottle an extra squeeze to squirt out about twice as much, indulging my morning petulance with extra calories.

"How are you feeling?" Matt asked, buttering his French toast.

"Like I want my normal boring life back." I cut into my French toast and speared a bite on the tines of my fork.

Chuckling, he shook his head. "Em, your life has never been normal or boring. I know you like to think it is, but it's not."

"Well, it was normal-er and boring-ish," I muttered in between bites of food. "This is delicious, thanks. But shouldn't you be at work?"

"It's Sunday."

"Oh. Right."

"Anyway, I wanted to talk to you, so I'm glad Dan made himself scarce."

I smirked. "Yeah. Making himself scarce seems to be his thing, these days."

Matt said nothing to defend my brother. He didn't really know him, after all, his only experience being limited to the previous night's events.

"Be that as it may..." He paused to bite into a piece of bacon that he'd dragged through the syrup on his plate. "You've been through a lot in the last few days. Particularly in the last twenty-four hours. It might be a good idea to take a few minutes to stop and assess."

"Ah, yes, the voice of reason." I eyed him over the rim of my coffee mug as I took another sip. "I'm afraid if I do that I might end up in a quivering ball of uselessness."

"That's what I'm here for." He smiled gently.

"To be a quivering ball of uselessness?"

Chuckling, he shook his head. "To make sure you don't stay one for too long. So, talk to me. How are you feeling? Really. Don't be flippant."

I sighed, pushing food around with my fork. "I don't know. Frustrated, I guess. Scared. A little angry."

"Why?"

"Because I don't understand what's going on, and all this time I thought I was just... a null, you know? Powerless."

"Hmm." He made all pretense of studying his plate, continuing to eat while he listened rather than watching me. He knew I hated it when people just watched me during conversations. "But you've never been a 'null,' not really. You can sense magic in others, see it when it's being used. You're not completely magic blind."

"All witches can do that."

"So, that makes you a witch, right? Even though you can't cast spells or whatever."

"I don't know, Matt. I just don't know anymore. I thought I had it all figured out, but this throws everything into chaos. I feel like I'm spiraling out of control with nothing to hold on to."

His fingers brushed my forearm, curling over it briefly to give a supportive squeeze. "You have me."

I smiled, weakly. "I know, thanks." I gave his hand a pat, then went back to eating. "I just wish I knew what was going on."

"We'll figure it out. I promise."

For some dumb reason, I believed him.

Dan showed up while we were finishing up, breezing into the apartment far too cheerfully. "Good morning, sis!

Good morning, Matt! Oh good, you're just about done. We have to go."

Matt and I both looked at him warily. He beat me to replying. "We?"

"Well, Em and me. We have a meeting with Detective Escobar." Dan flopped on the couch and put his feet up on the coffee table, making himself at home. He had quite the nest of blankets and pillows there. Matt must have set him up the previous night before coming to bed.

"We do?" I asked, eyeing him from afar. Warily.

"Yeah." He tossed something onto the coffee table. It landed with a thud.

My eyes narrowed. "Is that my phone?"

"Huh? Oh, yeah. I figured you wouldn't leave without it while I was gone. Who's Barry, by the way? He wants to get together for coffee."

I was gritting my teeth already, and it was barely 9:00 a.m. "None of your business." I pushed my chair back abruptly and began collecting the breakfast plates from the table. By long-standing agreement, Matt cooks and I do dishes.

"Wait, isn't your cat named Barry?"

"Lord Barrington would not suffer a peasant addressing him so familiarly," Matt said, but the damage was done. Barry. Barrington. Why hadn't I made that connection sooner, and was the mental image of my would-be suitor licking himself going to haunt me forever?

I turned on the water, drowning out further conversation in my immediate vicinity, but I didn't have much to wash. It was done all too quickly.

"I'm going to grab a shower." I paused on my way past Matt and gave his shoulder a squeeze. "Thanks for the chat. Text me later. I promise I'll answer."

Dan sat up a little on the couch, craning his neck to look over the arm of it toward me. "No time, sis! We have to go!"

"If Escobar calls, tell him I had to take a shower," I said, waving him off. If he liked playing secretary so much, I'd leave him to it.

"Okay, what should I tell Barry?" I heard him call as I was on the way down the hall. I pretended not to hear him.

CHAPTER 20

I thought Escobar's eyes were going to pop out of his head when I walked into Rocky's Roasters with Dan. He was sitting at one of the tiny round tables so popular in coffee shops that want to discourage people from busting out their laptops and hunkering down. I definitely needed more coffee to face the music, so I waved to Escobar and herded Dan toward the counter. I'm sure Escobar wanted answers, but he was going to have to wait a couple of minutes. Or a "cuppa" minutes, if you prefer. Har-har.

By the time we made our way to the table where Escobar was sitting, he'd had plenty of time to compose himself and think about how he wanted to start the conversation. That may have been a misstep on my part.

"Hey, sorry we're late. Um, are we late?" I glanced over at Dan, who pushed back the sleeve of his coat to display his bare wrist.

"No idea."

I looked back at Escobar and shrugged, slipping into one of the chairs. Dan spun the other around and proceeded to sit backwards in it, a move that made Escobar shift in his own chair, sitting a little straighter. I got the feeling I was missing out on some sort of guy thing, but I didn't ask.

"So, who's your friend?" Escobar asked, taking an all too casual sip from his cup.

"Down to business. Right. This is my brother, Daniel. Daniel, this is Detective Michael Escobar, SFPD's Magic Crimes lead."

Dan grimaced. "Please, call me Dan." He reached across the table to offer the detective a handshake.

Escobar stared at the offered hand for a few seconds before leaning forward and accepting the handshake. Some pretty intense eye contact was made, or at least attempted, on Escobar's part. Dan was as irreverent as ever, just smiling and almost immediately getting distracted by a pretty girl across the room.

I rolled my eyes and took a careful sip of my coffee. It was hot, so I put it back down again. "Look, I know I've got some explaining to do."

Escobar grunted, shifting his attention from Dan to me. "I'll say."

"I know, it was shitty of me not to say anything, but it would have been shitty of me to turn him over, too. He's my brother. I never thought he had anything to do with this, and now I can prove it."

"I'd love to hear this one," Escobar murmured around another sip of java.

"He was with me last night when the witch was attacked. So, he definitely wasn't behind it. He's got an alibi now."

"Mmm-hmm. He does. For one of the attacks. Assuming it wasn't orchestrated to give him one."

Frowning, I eyed him from across the table. "There were witnesses."

"All of whom left the scene before I got there. Including

this one." He pointed at Dan. "The only thing I have is contact info for a single witch that supposedly put a binding on the victim." There was a little too much skepticism in there for my taste. But as a cop he was trained to question things, to take nothing at face value.

I sighed. "What do you want from me?"

"Well, for one I'd like to be able to trust you. But you're really putting me in a bind there."

"I'm sorry. But he can help. He knows way more about this shit than I do. The homunculus was his idea."

"It was also the wrong idea. He could've been throwing us off his tracks."

"He's also sitting right here," Dan said with a smirk. "If you want to arrest me, arrest me. Otherwise, put me to work or tell me to buzz off. I've got better things to do."

I strongly doubted that, but I wasn't about to point it out. Escobar and I both eyed him, and whatever was on our faces made Dan laugh suddenly.

"Ha-ha, you two should date."

I scowled and refrained from throwing perfectly good coffee in his face. Won't say I wasn't tempted, though.

"She's a little mouthy for my taste," Escobar said dryly, and this time it was my turn to laugh.

"Aw, shucks. You're too kind." I batted my eyes at him. He ignored me and lifted his coffee for another sip. I went on. "But seriously. Bring him on to consult. Let him help. He's a pain in the ass, but he knows his shit."

"You really need to work on your flattery," Dan said. I elbowed him in the ribs. It actually shut him up, and I made a mental note to remember that tactic.

Meanwhile, Escobar sighed and shook his head. "No way is the chief going to sign off on another consultant."

"We can share the consultant fee," I said.

Dan straightened in his chair. "You're getting paid?"

Escobar made a thoughtful noise and glanced up at the ceiling. "I might be able to make that happen. But first, he's going to have to prove his worth." Pushing back his chair, he collected his cup and got to his feet. "Come on, gumshoes. We've got an interview to conduct."

Dan hummed the *Where in the World is Carmen Sandiego* song as we exited the coffee shop. It was going to be a long day.

CHAPTER 21

The motel that the SFPD put Gabriel up in was definitely no-frills. There were a pair of uniforms in a patrol car parked in the lot outside, and another one actually in the room with Gabriel when we got there. She looked a little happy to be relieved by Escobar, even if it was only for a little while. Gabriel was awake, sitting on the bed and playing solitaire with an old deck of red-backed playing cards.

I'd seen the spiderweb of wards the moment the door was opened and hesitated outside, much as I had when I first encountered the warded room Christina was kept in. Dan did too, studying the wards with a more critical eye.

"We can't go in there," he said.

Inside, Escobar turned to look out at us. "Why not?"

"Because we're not keyed to it. It's set up to keep magic users, creatures, constructs, and spells out. I could probably force my way in, but that would shatter them."

I stepped up beside Dan and reached out to touch the glimmering web across the doorway, skimming my fingertips against it. I felt it react to me with the strange sort of cool elasticity that was an exact mirror of the wards protecting Christina. I pushed and my hand passed through. I moved forward, slipping through with a shiver and a glance over my shoulder as the wards rebounded back into place. Dan stood on the other side, mouth agape. He reached out the way that I had, but when he pushed against the wards they didn't budge, and his hand failed to pass through.

"I guess you're going to have to wait out there." I flashed him a smile and closed the door in his face. It wasn't very big of me, but it was satisfying. I was still smiling when I turned back to look around the room. It was poorly lit, a little dingy, and smelled of stale cigarette smoke. No matter how vigorously you scrubbed, it was difficult to get out, and I was pretty sure this room hadn't been vigorously scrubbed in years, anyway.

"Mr. Sanchez, I'm glad to see you're doing well. I'm Detective Escobar and this is my associate, Emily Davenport. We're here to ask you a few questions."

Gabriel looked up briefly, then went back to his game, continuing to flip the cards from the stock pile over three at a time. "That's great. I have a few for you too."

I moved over to lean against the dresser, preferring standing to sitting for the moment. "We'll do our best to answer them," I said, not wanting to be left out entirely. Escobar shot me a warning look, but I shrugged and went quiet again, letting him take the lead. Which one of us was supposed to be the good cop? I wasn't sure. Then again, this was an interview, not an interrogation.

"Can you walk me through the events from last night?" Escobar began, taking out one of those tiny notepads and flipping through a few pages before finding a clean one to take notes on. It was so analog I had to smile.

"Not really, the last thing I remember before waking up in the ambulance was walking down the street. I was on my way to a meeting."

Escobar glanced up from his notepad, curiously. "What kind of meeting?"

"Alcoholics Anonymous." As he spoke, Gabriel kept playing, moving the cards around atop the comforter into neat little piles.

There was a nod from the detective, along with a brief scribble on the notepad. "There was nothing unusual at all, no warning? You were just walking along and the next thing you remember is waking up in the ambulance?"

"Yeah, it was damned strange. Unnerving." He flipped through the last few cards in the stock pile several times in rapid succession, then started gathering up the cards to shuffle. Apparently he'd lost the game.

"Okay, let's work backwards then," Escobar said. "What did you do before you left for the meeting? Where were you? Did anything seem strange?"

I had a feeling we weren't going to get much from this interview, and I was right. Gabriel had a pretty average Saturday. He went to the bank, did some chores around the house for his family, watched a football game, pretty normal stuff, all in all.

"So, how long am I going to have to stay cooped up here?" he asked after a while.

"Until we can be sure you're no longer in danger," Escobar replied.

Gabriel grimaced. "My old lady's not gonna like that. Can you call her? Phone in here isn't working."

Much like the lights, the television... no wonder he was playing solitaire.

"She's been notified, as has your employer. Really, all you need to do is hang tight and let us figure this out."

Telling a bound witch in a warded room to hang tight is an exercise in futility, but on the whole, Gabriel seemed to be handling it pretty well.

"Take your time," he said. "I mean, it sucks not being able to watch TV, but I haven't slept this well in years."

At least someone was content with the situation.

Dan was leaning against the wall outside when we emerged, casually flirting with the police officer that we'd relieved when we went in. I admit I'd hoped he'd be moping like a petulant child. The uniformed woman was a little thick around the middle and obviously flattered to have the attention of a young, attractive man. Before we left, she wrote her phone number on the palm of his hand with a ballpoint pen, making eyes at him like a teenager. Escobar shot me a glance, and I rolled my eyes, grabbed Dan's arm and dragged him away.

"Call me!" the woman called after us.

Dan grinned as I propelled him along.

"Do you ever think about anything but getting your dick wet?" I growled through gritted teeth.

"Oh, come on. Doris seems like a very nice woman." Doris, like something out of Leave it to Beaver. Wholesome, Americana. Somehow it made me feel even worse for her.

"I'm sure she is. That's just one of the umpteen reasons I can think of, off the top of my head, for you to stay the hell away from her."

"Jealous? You know, if things don't work out with Baryou could give you a few pointers."

"Shut up."

He did, but it didn't stop me from wanting to wipe the smug smile off his face all the way back to the car.

Escobar had parked next to us. He paused to wait for us to catch up, saying once we were in range, "I'm going to head back to the station and see what I can do about pretty boy, here. Want to meet me there in a couple of hours? We can go over what we've got with Danny boy."

Pretty boy. Danny boy. I expected him to object, but Dan just smiled and chirped, "Sounds good, Detective!"

I eyed Dan but nodded my agreement. "Yeah, that's fine." I unlocked the car and Dan wasted no time getting in.

"Emily," Escobar said, motioning me closer with his head while he slipped a hand inside his coat.

Curious, I moved closer. "Yeah?"

He removed a plain white envelope from an inner coat pocket and offered it to me. "Think about it."

I looked down at the envelope, then back at him, but he was already turning away to get into his car. By the time I fumbled the envelope open with my gloved hands and unfolded the pages within, he'd already started the engine and was backing out of the parking place.

It was a very official-looking document, with the New Mexico state seal adorning the top left corner of the first page. Beside it, the bold heading read: **Application for Admission to the New Mexico State Registry for Magic Practitioners**

Subtle, Escobar. Real subtle.

CHAPTER 22

"What's that?" Dan asked as I settled into the driver's seat with the envelope in my hand.

"Nothing." I stuffed the envelope behind the sun visor and started the car. While the car warmed up, I tugged off a glove and whipped out my phone.

Dan watched me for a moment, but let it go. "So, what now?"

"I was thinking lunch. How does that sound?" I asked, eyes still focused on the little rectangular screen.

"Lunch sounds... good?" He must have expected something else, because his reply had a hint of suspicion in it.

His suspicion was well-placed. Once I had answered assorted messages, I sent a fresh one off to a certain coven leader, tucked my phone away, and got us on the road.

Business at the Tin Whistle was booming when we got there, like I'd hoped. I didn't see Hector's truck in the parking lot, but that didn't mean the witch wasn't skulking around somewhere. Fortunately, the lunch rush was just getting started, so the line wasn't quite out the door yet.

As we made our way inside, Dan looked around curiously. "This place is pretty cool. You come here often?"

"Yeah. Menu's on the board over the counter. Figure out what you want while we wait."

While he studied the menu, I looked around the crowded restaurant, observing the usual crop of locals. My eyes skimmed the artwork on the walls by habit. It cycled regularly, since all the pieces were for sale. I noticed there was a new painting hanging on the far wall, near the bathrooms. Earthy browns, oranges, and reds zig-zagged across the canvas which was full of angles in a very modern style. The subject was very natural, though: an arid valley with a stream stretching from the foreground into the background, bending sharply as it flowed toward a distant horizon.

Dan noticed my distraction when I didn't move forward with him as the line crept along. He backtracked and leaned down, looking over my shoulder to try and figure out what I was looking at.

"Daddy issues?" he asked, breaking me out of my reverie.

"Huh?" I glanced over at him in confusion, then frowned and moved forward to close the gap in the line before there was any impatient throat-clearing or eager lunch-goers cutting in front of us.

"That guy over there."

I looked. Hey, there *was* a guy sitting under the painting, an older guy in a company-branded polo shirt with a full head of silver hair and the telltale spark of a magic user. Eyes on his plate, he ate with the steady cadence of a man on a schedule. He was a regular, though as is often the case with urban dwellers crossing paths around the city, I didn't know him by name. Smirking, I rolled my eyes and turned my attention elsewhere again. "I wasn't looking at him, I was looking at the painting."

"Oh." Beside me, Dan focused on the painting for a moment before moving on. "I guess it's okay."

Okay, he said. I'd been completely drawn in to that breathtaking work of art. I'd had a moment. But to him it was just okay.

Feeling a little vindictive, turned my attention back to my brother. "Maybe I'll take you by the Jackalope later. I think it's more your speed."

"Jackalope? Is that some local pumpkin thing? Or a bar?" He sounded hopeful at the thought of a bar.

"Pumpkin thing?" I blinked over at him, uncomprehendingly.

"You know, like Halloween. Jack-o-Lantern, Jackalope. Never mind. What's a jackalope?"

"It's a rabbit with antlers. But I was talking about the store. It sells all kinds of artisan goods, locally crafted and imported from Mexico." Tourist. Trap.

"Oh, okay."

I sighed. It wasn't quite as much fun insulting him when he didn't know I was doing it.

"Those don't really exist, do they?" he asked after a pause. "Rabbits with antlers? That sounds almost as terrifying as the ones from Monty Python with nasty big pointy teeth."

"Only in folklore, as far as I know. Did you make up your mind yet?"

The last person in front of us was clearing out of the way, and from behind the counter Penny the barista chirped, "Hey, Emily! Haven't seen you in a few days. Who's your friend?"

The young woman eyed my brother in open appreciation. I could almost feel him puffing up beside me, but when I glanced his way he was playing it cool. I caught him winking at her though. This was really getting old.

"My brother. Don't get too excited. He's unemployed and has a kid on the way."

Beside me, Dan made a strangled noise and started coughing. Finally! Got him.

Penny laughed. "Fair enough. Well, good luck with the job search. We're hiring a busboy, but I don't imagine that's what you're looking for."

I perked. "Really? I wouldn't rule it out. Could we have an application?" I spared another glance over at Dan. His face was turning a lovely shade of pink.

Penny obliged, fishing a pre-printed application pad out from under the counter and tearing the top page off to slide across the counter. I thanked her, then got on with the business of ordering rather than tormenting my brother further. Once she'd given us a number for our table, we headed off to find one.

"So, you're really not going to tell me what's in that envelope? Was it the consulting fee? You said you'd share," Dan said, sliding into a chair. He seemed to have mostly recovered from the embarrassment at the counter.

"It's not money, and trust me, you don't want any part in it." I studied him thoughtfully for a moment, frowning to myself. "Then again, you might get presented with one yourself if you stick around town."

"Was it a restraining order? Because I'm only like six states shy of a full set," he quipped, draping an arm over the back of his chair and slumping down a bit. The man made slumping an art form, I swear.

"Do you ever take anything seriously?"

"I try not to. It's really boring. What was in the envelope? Now I *have* to know."

Sighing, I reached for the salt shaker on the table and fiddled with it, accidentally knocking it over. Salt spilled across the table, and I winced, pinched a bit, and threw it over my shoulder. I'm not that superstitious, but the way things were going lately… it couldn't hurt. "It was an application for the state registry."

"State reg— Ohhhh. You told him about what happened, eh?" Grimacing, he shook his head.

"Of course I did. I had to." Frowning, I set the salt shaker back in the caddy, tucking it in beside the pepper.

"I wouldn't have."

"Yeah, but evasion and obfuscation come naturally to you. Some of us have to work at it."

"Thank you."

"It wasn't a compliment."

Fortunately, our food arrived quickly so the conversation was fairly brief. I had ordered soup and half a sandwich, while he had ordered a burger and fries.

I looked between our plates. "Do you work out?" I couldn't help but ask.

"Not really," he said around a mouthful of cheeseburger. Naturally.

I changed the subject again. "Okay, so if you're going to be staying at my place for a while, we're going to need some ground rules."

"You know I love rules," he commented, mouth still full. That was sarcasm, for those following along at home.

"I'm serious. First, stay out of my room. You've got full run of the rest of the apartment, but that's my space." I pointed my spoon at him for emphasis.

"Alright, what else?"

"No pranks. I don't want to end up glued to the toilet seat or trying to fry hard-boiled eggs in the morning."

He snickered a little, no doubt recalling these and other things from our childhood. But he nodded his head in acquiescence, nonetheless.

"No girls. If you're going to hook up, do it somewhere else."

I thought he was going to protest that, but he merely smirked and nodded again. This was going better than I expected.

"Last but not least... you need to get a job."

His eyes went wide and he set his burger down. "Whaaaat? Oh, come on..."

"Don't 'oh come on' me. You don't have to be a busboy, but you need to do something. I'm not going to slave away at work all day while you sit around the house eating cereal from the box and watching TV. It'll be good for you. Work builds character."

He groaned. "Ugh. God, you're channeling Dad."

I reached across the table and stole a French fry from his plate. "Yeah, just be glad it's not Mother."

Dan drummed his fingertips on the table, watching me for a moment. A long, calculating moment. "Define 'job'?"

"Um. A task you perform, legally and preferably out of the house, for which you receive payment, minus state and federal withholdings."

"Okay," he said, quickly enough that it gave me pause.

I was still trying to figure out what the loophole in my definition was when a familiar voice said from behind me, "Well, what do we have here?"

I glanced back, flashing Tall Dark and Witchy a smile. "Hey, Hector, fancy meeting you here."

Across the table, Dan looked like he was having a fight-

or-flight moment. His fingers gripped the edge of the table and he had his chair half pushed back.

I lifted my brows and made a downward gesture with my spoon. "Oh no, you don't. You and Hector are going to hash this out by the time I finish my lunch, because I'm tired of being caught in the middle. Hector, grab a chair."

Power flared around Hector, a glowing nimbus of magical energy wrapping around him. He cast a tentacle-like magical appendage out to float a chair across the short distance between the nearest empty table and ours. It happened quickly enough that it turned a few heads, but the mundies quickly went back to their meals, probably uncertain if they'd really seen it happen. He really must have been fired-up to make such an open display in a public place. But he used his hand to spin the chair around and straddled it, parking his narrow behind on the padded cushion.

Dan had actually flinched when Hector started to cast, but he recovered quickly and seemed to relax again, picking up his burger and biting into it as though he weren't concerned at all about Hector's presence. Say what you will about my brother, he has great big titanium balls. It's a wonder he can walk, much less sit comfortably.

"It's so good to see you again, Daniel," Hector said, a little too warmly.

"Dan," my brother corrected, automatically. "And you too, I guess. How's Christina?"

"So kind of you to show concern. She is as well as can be expected, under the circumstances." Hector folded his arms along the top of the chair back. "Your sister has been quite adamant that you had nothing to do with what happened to her and Tori. I'll admit, I wasn't inclined to believe her."

"Well, you should. Because I didn't," Dan said, but I

picked up on something he missed, and it had my intention more focused on Hector than before.

"Oh? What happened to change your mind?" I asked.

He smiled. "Oh, nothing. Well, a little something I suppose. A little birdie whispered in my ear. I found what she had to say very interesting." Again, that telltale glow sprung to life around Hector. Tendrils of power rose from the floor behind Dan, reaching up to toy with him. One tapped him on the shoulder, and when he glanced back it tapped his other shoulder.

Once he figured out what Hector was up to, he rolled his eyes. "What are you, twelve? Gah, not the hair!" He reached up to swat at the unseen force, but his hands just passed through it ineffectually.

Hector laughed but relented. He even stopped casting, throwing back his head and laughing loudly enough to draw attention from nearby tables. I met at least one pair of eyes and made the universal symbol for "crazy" with my index finger pointing at my head.

"So it's true, you really are bound. Who was it? A jealous lover? Jealous husband? Parole officer? Jealous parole officer?" Hector was enjoying this way too much. If anyone was going to make fun of my little brother, it'd be me.

While Dan shot daggers at Hector with his eyes, I played the big sister card and stepped in. "Hector, don't be an ass. Do you actually want to talk about anything, or just gloat?"

"Mostly just gloat," he admitted. "But if it helps, your brother here can consider himself cleared in the eyes of the coven."

"Do I even want to know what little bird whispered that to you?" I asked, genuinely curious.

"I wouldn't tell you if you asked," Hector said, getting to his feet.

"Wait." Dan looked up at Hector with a pained expression. "I know you don't like me, and I guess you've got good enough reason for that, but we're all on the same side here. Do you think maybe you could help a brother out?"

Hector leaned over, putting his hands on the table and looking into Dan's eyes. The expression on his face shifted from amused and carefree to hard as a rock in the span of a heartbeat. "You are not my brother, and I wouldn't undo your binding if God himself asked me to. Save your breath, Daniel. You're going to need it to scream when Joseph catches up to you."

Dan frowned but didn't shrink in the slightest. "I don't even know what his problem is. Nothing happened between me and Christina."

"Neither do I," Hector replied. "But I don't really give a shit." With that said, he turned and walked away, heading for the exit.

I watched him go, then looked back at my brother who seemed to have lost some of his appetite. "Can I have some of those pointers now, oh great and wise social guru?" I asked, stealing another French fry.

Sometimes I just can't help myself.

CHAPTER 23

Dan and I spent the rest of the day at the police station, poring over evidence with Escobar. What little evidence we had, anyway. By this time, we'd managed to build a rough timeline for each incident. The photos of all the witches, dead or not, were posted up on a whiteboard in the squad room, along with whatever tenuous connections we had been able to come up with between them. I'd tried to put Escobar's old partner on the board, but for whatever reason, he wouldn't let me—not until we could link her to the others in some meaningful way, or somehow prove that she'd burned out before she died. It's a really hard thing to prove after the fact, so I had a feeling we might never know for sure.

For the most part, our victims were as different as any random sampling of the population might be. The only thing they seemed to have in common was that they were all witches. Only two, Tori and Christina, were in the same coven. We weren't sure if William Hines was in a coven, but Gabriel Sanchez wasn't. Most witches belong to some sort of coven, even if it's more of a family thing the way the Davenport Coven is. There's safety in numbers, after all. But witches can be loners like anyone else, and not every witch is lucky enough to have a whole family of practitioners to support and teach them either. When two witch parents have a child, that child is a witch. I used to think I was an exception to that rule, but after the previous night all bets were off.

When a witch and a mundane have a child, it's almost always mundane—that's why my mom was so pissed at Dan, and why she resented my existence so much. The Davenport bloodline can be traced back to Salem, and to the Old World before that. But that... whatever it is that makes a witch a witch... it can pop up randomly from two seemingly mundane parents if either of them has a little witch blood in their family tree.

It was late when Dan and I got home. He'd actually proven himself pretty helpful over the course of the afternoon, and his arcane knowledge was more impressive than I expected. He'd spent a couple of hours just brainstorming, considering the types of spells that might do what was being done, and how they'd be performed, just to try and give us a better idea of what we were up against. He was convinced that it was a person, not a creature, that was behind all of this. I was inclined to believe him. The question was, what kind of awful person would pull so much magic through a witch that it would burn them out? Was it intentional, or a side effect? And what exactly were they doing with all that ill-gotten magic? We had a lot of questions, but precious few answers.

We were running out of time, and I could feel the pressure mounting. How long would the assailant wait before giving up on Gabriel and moving on to someone else? Had it happened already? How could we protect anyone without knowing when or where they might strike next?

Dan chattered at me all the way home, but I barely heard a word he said. By the time we made it into the apartment, all I wanted was to be alone. I hadn't been alone for longer than a bathroom break in over twelve hours, so I dumped the files on the dining table and gave Dan instructions for feeding Barrington on my way down the hall. I dumped my coat, gloves, and scarf on the floor as I made my way across the bedroom to face-plant on the bed. My phone started buzzing almost immediately, and I had to resist the urge to hurl it across the room. What if it was important?

"Hello?" I probably sounded both weary and wary. It was an unknown number.

"Hi, could I speak to Emily please?"

"Speaking."

"Oh, hi Emily. This is John Warren. We met last night?" It wasn't a super familiar voice, but the list of men I'd met the previous night was short. Only one of them had ended up with my phone number. Okay, so really there was only one of them on the list to start with.

It was the witch, the one that had come to our rescue and cast the binding on Gabriel. "Ahh, right. What's up?" I rolled over onto my back and pushed at the heel of one shoe with the toe of the other to pry it off. It landed on the wooden floor with a quiet thud.

"I was just wondering what became of the man last night. Is he okay? I could sense him for a while, but then he just... vanished."

Witches could sense others they'd bound? That was interesting. It also meant that, even bound and banished, my brother was still there lurking in the back of our mother's mind, like an itch that wouldn't go away. That seemed fitting. Poetic justice, if nothing else.

"Yeah, he's fine. We've got him in a warded room. That's probably why you can't sense him anymore." I pushed the other shoe off and wiggled my toes, feet still hanging off the edge of the bed.

"Oh, okay. Well, I'm glad," he said, and there was a bit of an awkward pause afterward.

"Was there something else?" I admit I was a little intrigued by the fellow. What was his story? What had made him come forward when others hurried away?

"Oh. Uh, no. I mean, maybe. I'm kind of curious about what you did to him. I've never seen anyone do anything like that before."

"Yeah, you and me both. I've never done anything like that before. It just kind of happened."

"Oh, I see. That's very interesting." There was an unmistakable note of speculation in his voice. "Would you like to see if you can do it again?"

My brows went up. "Is that an invitation?" It hadn't occurred to me to try it again; the incident had scared the piss out of me. I wasn't even sure if I *could* do it again on demand.

"It could be," he said, backing away from the commitment a little bit. "There's someone I'd like to introduce you to. She might be able to help. She's a very wise woman. Knows many things, has seen many things."

I was somehow both tempted and wary all at the same time. "I don't know..."

"It's up to you. In fact, consider it an open invitation. You've got my number." I liked that he didn't put the screws to me or anything. Most of the men in my life are just so damn pushy. "Anyway, I'll let you go."

I hesitated a moment, then said, "John?"

"Yeah?"

"What about what was happening with Gabriel? The man we rescued. Have you ever seen something like *that* before?" It never hurt to ask.

"Only in nightmares."

"No prophetic tendencies, I hope?"

He chuckled, and I smiled in spite of myself. "Nope. But if I develop any, I'll let you know."

"It was really great of you to help. You didn't have to do it, and I just— Thank you."

"Running into burning buildings is kind of my thing. Take it easy, Emily."

"You too." I hung up and dropped the phone onto the bed beside me, stretching out and lacing my fingers together behind my head. I lay there for the better part of an hour, staring up at the ceiling and letting my mind wander until I heard a light, timid knock at my door.

"Yeah?" I turned my head to look in the direction of the door. It cracked open a little, and Dan peeked in.

"Can I come in?" He pushed the door open a little bit wider, daring to look around my Fortress of Solitude.

I sighed. "Yeah. But this isn't a standing invitation, just a temporary suspension of the roommate accord." I gave the bed beside me a pat. "What's up?"

Pushing the door open the rest of the way, he wandered into the room, stepping around the various articles of clothing on the floor and coming to sit on the bed beside me.

"Look, I've been thinking, and I want you to know that I'm not going to tell Mom or Dad about last night. What you did."

"Oh?" I eyed him, the subject still a bit sore. "What brought about that change of heart?"

He shrugged, looking down at the comforter. "Nothing, really. I never intended to follow through with it. Sometimes I say things without really thinking it through, you know?"

"Uh-huh."

"Shut up, I'm trying to be genuine here." He poked me in the side.

"Uh-huh."

"Anyway, it was shitty of me, and I'm sorry. I just want to help, and this damn binding... You have no idea what it's like, Em. If I don't get it off, I'm going to go crazy."

"Did you really think Hector would do it for you?" I'd been wondering about that off and on ever since the incident with the coven leader earlier in the day.

"No. But he's the only one I've come across that's strong enough since I got here. It's not like this podunk town is overflowing with powerful witches."

"Why do you think I like it?" I smiled and poked his leg. One good poke deserves another, after all.

"I don't know, honestly. It's like living on another planet, compared to back home. Weird people, weird customs. If there weren't a Starbucks I'd think we were on Mars or something."

"I'm pretty sure there's a Starbucks opening on Mars next year," I joked, earning a faint smile from him. I pushed myself up into a sitting position, folding my legs Indian style. "I know this is tough for you, and I'll do what I can to find someone to get your binding off. In the meantime, you just need to... I don't know. Grow up."

He glanced at me, flashing me a wounded look. I guess I could have been gentler about it. But I felt like it needed to be said. "Sorry. What I mean is quit acting like everything's a big joke and take things more seriously. That's what got you into this mess to start with, remember?"

He grimaced, but at least he wasn't laughing me off. He was listening, which was a step in the right direction as far as I was concerned.

"Alright," he said. "I'll try."

I reached over and drew him into a hug, and he leaned against me for a long moment. In that moment, I saw the mask fall away and realized that underneath all his bravado and buffoonery he was deeply wounded. I knew how that felt, even if I was still a little irked at him over the whole "abandoning a pregnant woman" thing. Anyway, I hugged him tighter for a few moments more but let him go when he pulled away.

"Enough about me," he said, scratching his chin. He had a couple of days' worth of scruff going on. "Let's talk about you."

And things were going so well. I groaned, drawing my knees up to half-mast and looping my arms around them loosely. "Do we have to?"

"Yes. We need to talk about what happened last night, what you did. That was incredible."

"Well, I don't like to brag." It might be possible that there is a smart-ass gene that runs in my family. In others, it's an annoyance. In me, I don't mind it so much.

"That's not what I mean. I mean incredible as in not believable. That shouldn't be possible. I've never even heard of it." My jovial baby brother was suddenly very serious. I wasn't sure if I liked it. "What else can you do?"

"Huh? Nothing, at least not that I know of. I've never done anything like it before, and the whole family knows I have no magical ability. I'm The Null, remember?" Even from my own lips, the word stung.

At least he grimaced. Point for him. "Well, you could see the wards at the motel, right?"

I shrugged. "Yeah, but so can you."

"So that means you're not a null. What else can you do?"

"Um... I can see any magic that's being slung around, and I can sense witches."

His head came up, blue eyes focusing on me intensely. "You can sense witches? Even when they're not actively using magic?"

"Yeah, can't you?"

"No, that's not something witches can do. At least, not that I know of..." He trailed off, looking at me thoughtfully.

I repressed the urge to squirm. "Okay, so maybe I'm witch-adjacent. Now what?"

"Well, you're going to need a crash course in magic. You never got the same lessons we did, did you?"

I smirked, shaking my head. "No, there wasn't any point since I didn't have any ability. I learned a little bit. Whatever I happened to overhear."

"I don't have any of the references we'll need. Maybe Liam could—"

"No!" I straightened abruptly. "I don't want to involve the family in this."

"Yeah, I had a feeling you were going to say that. Maybe the locals can be of some help?" he suggested, hopefully.

I looked away, thinking about the conversation I'd just had with John Warren. "I don't really want to tell anyone that we don't have to. I mean, what if this is just the tip of the iceberg? What if I become dangerous?"

"You're an untrained witch. You're already dangerous." At least he tried to be gentle about it, laying a hand on my knee. "Liam has access to the family library. He can do some research. I don't even have to tell him that it's about you, I can just... ask some general questions. You know what he's like. If he gets curious enough, he'll throw himself into research mode, and who knows what he might find."

"Yeah, but if he doesn't have the context, he won't know that it's important he shares what he finds." I picked at a stray thread on my comforter, glancing up at him again after a moment's pause. "There may be another way."

"Oh? What's that?"

"You know that witch that rode to the rescue last night? He called, said he knows someone that might be able to help."

"That's probably code for his penis."

I grabbed a pillow and swatted him with it. He grinned, throwing an arm up in self-defense. An hour ago I would have found it infuriating, but now... I don't know. Something had shifted, some realignment in our relationship. Years' worth of animosity can't be undone in an hour, but I was making progress.

"You're disgusting," I said, but less seriously than I might have before.

"Do what you're good at, right?" But his grin faded after a few seconds. He looked at me thoughtfully and said, "Do whatever you think you need to do. Just, uh, if you do go visit some wizened old Indian woman, ask if she has any good fry bread recipes. That shit is delicious."

"Out, get out!" I pointed imperiously at the door, but he had me laughing in spite of myself, and that laughter eased the knot of emotions in my chest. Sometimes laughter *is* the best medicine.

CHAPTER 24

The next morning found me driving down an unnamed dirt road in the foothills north of the city, somewhere in the ass-end of the Pojoaque Pueblo. There's a reason why I own a four-wheel drive, and this technically wasn't it, but it was a good reason for me to be glad for it. The roads out there didn't get plowed. They only remained passable thanks to the traffic of the people that lived there. More than once, my tires slipped on ice, but I managed to stay on the road.

Also more than once, I had to squint at the directions I'd been given. That's the thing about unnamed roads. There's not an abundance of landmarks. I was pretty sure even Amazon didn't deliver out here. Maybe someday the drones would. I finally spotted the red gate I'd been advised to look for, and another quarter-mile down the road was the turnoff I was supposed to take.

As I bounced along down the winding road, I started to reconsider my decision to come out here alone. Bringing Dan would have been... well, not smarter, but it would have been nice to have some backup. I did call Matt before I left, though, so at least someone else knew where I'd gone. I'd dropped Dan off at the police station before I left town so he could run interference with Escobar and maybe get some work done while I was out. I wasn't expecting them to have any major breakthroughs, but it at least made me feel a little better about taking this time to run a very personal errand.

The blue fence was easy to spot against a white backdrop. It was a tall privacy fence; all I could see of the house behind it was the roof. There was a beat-up old pickup truck parked next to the gate. I parked beside the truck. The snow there looked untouched, whereas it was clear that the truck moved in and out of its parking spot regularly. I hoped it was actually another parking spot I'd taken and not just a wintering garden or something. Hi John, thanks for your help, sorry I flattened your tubers. That'd be awkward.

Climbing out of the car, I took a closer look around. The landscape was covered in a fresh dusting of snow from last night. This far out of the city, it was peaceful and quiet. The air was cleaner, crisper somehow. And the land, it just felt older. It's nonsense, of course, but there's something about a less-developed area—it always seems older to me, like it has maintained something that more urban landscapes have lost. A sense of the past, of the wildness that still exists in pockets like these across the world.

On the other side of the fence, a dog barked when I closed my car door. It was the low, deep bark of a large dog, but not a very enthusiastic one. I couldn't help but think of it as more of a heads-up than a sound to warn off would-be trespassers. The snow crunched under my boots as I made my way to the gate.

"Wear sensible shoes," he'd said. Humph. Like I really need prompting for that. Shoes are one of my few true vanities, and I rather pride myself on my ability to select something appropriate to an occasion. Most days, that meant nursing shoes or sneakers. But when traipsing out into the wilderness on a snowy day something a little more rugged is called for. I didn't need some overbearing He-Man to tell me what to wear.

Anyhow, I peered through the narrow gap between the fence slats, trying to see if the dog was tied up or free-range. Before I could get a bead on it, or see much at all of the snow-covered yard beyond the fence, something blocked my view. I started slightly, chiding myself for being so distracted that I didn't notice a magical signature approaching. I knew it was John before he opened the gate, and when he did I flashed him a small smile.

He looked pretty much the same as I remembered him, wearing the same coat and what could have been the same pair of blue jeans. But let's face it, one pair of blue jeans can look pretty much like another. His long dark hair was tied back in a low ponytail at the base of his neck, somehow making his angular, handsome features all the more sharp. He smiled back at me, and for a moment I forgot to say anything.

"I hope the tribal police didn't give you any trouble?" he said, filling the gap I'd left easily enough. Today just so happened to be one of the Pueblo's two feast days, the only time during the year that it wasn't open to the public. The stores and museum were closed, and those seeking to soak in the community's history, arts, and crafts would have to wait a couple of days.

"Thankfully, no. I didn't even see any on the highway. I'm sorry to intrude on your feast day. We don't have to do this today if you don't want to. I can come back later in the week, or next week."

"Nonsense," he said, stepping outside the gate and

closing it behind him. Apparently, I wasn't going to get to peer into his life too closely on this trip. "We have some walking to do," he added, glancing briefly at my feet. But not so briefly that I didn't notice the glance.

Smirking, I lifted a foot and held it out for inspection. "Sensible, as requested." I couldn't keep the hint of sass out of my voice, but he didn't seem offended. More amused than anything, really.

"Didn't mean anything by it. Come on, we can walk and talk." He motioned for me to come with him and started walking down the drive past his truck, turning right eventually and starting to walk farther down the road. I went with him.

"Just so you know, I told people where I was going, so if you're planning to lure me out into the woods and axe me you'll have to be really careful about covering your tracks if you want to avoid prison time."

He laughed again, a quiet rumble from deep in his chest. "Thanks for the warning. I'm too pretty for prison," he joked, glancing up at the sky. Or, rather at the thick blanket of gray clouds that blocked the view of the sky.

I snickered softly, casting my gaze down the muddy road as we walked. "So, where are we going and why are we walking?" I kept my hands tucked in my pockets for warmth. It was cold enough that every exhale resulted in a puff of moist air.

"A good walk can clear the mind and purify the spirit," he said, suddenly sounding like some sort of tribal elder. He didn't look the part, couldn't have been much older than my twenty-eight years. "But really, not even my truck can get us where we need to go." He glanced at me with another smile.

"So, does that make this some kind of spirit walk?" I arched a brow.

He laughed, shaking his head. "I meant more in the literal sense. Kassidy's home is tucked away down an old game trail. It's too narrow for a vehicle to pass. She likes her solitude. In nicer weather, you could ride a bike, but today..." he gestured around at the snowy landscape. "I don't recommend it."

"Oh." I felt my cheeks pinken somewhat. "So, this Kassidy is the person you wanted me to meet?"

"Yes. She is... a singular woman. You'll see."

We made idle chit-chat the rest of the way. It must have been at least a mile on foot, over some tricky terrain thanks to ice and snow. John was sure-footed all the way, always with a quick hand ready to catch me if I stumbled over a rock or slipped on a slick patch of ice. I don't know quite what I expected to find at the other end of our journey... Okay, that's not true. I knew exactly what I expected to find: some ancient, crumbling adobe or sweat lodge in the middle of nowhere. Instead, it was an honest-to-goodness log cabin. The cabin was fairly small, maybe nine-hundred square feet total with enough room for one or two bedrooms depending on how large the common area was.

John led the way up the stairs out front. They were treated concrete, the sort that won't ice over, and judging from the layers of snow our shoes crunched into, no one had been up or down them for a while.

"Are you sure she's here?" I asked. There wasn't even a puff of smoke from either of the chimneys.

"Oh yes, she's always here." He flashed me a reassuring smile as he walked across the little porch in front and knocked lightly on the door. Even the welcome mat was covered in snow.

From the other side of the door, a woman's voice called, "Come in!"

John stomped his feet outside before opening the door and stepping inside. I followed his lead, comforted—if confused—by the warm air that greeted us. It was downright cozy inside the cabin, and I closed the door quickly behind me to keep the heat from escaping. Inside, the cabin had a sort of rustic-meets-homey vibe. Wood-paneled walls contrasted sharply with light airy curtains and woven throw rugs. There *was* a fire in the fireplace, the source of the room's heat. But there was something unnatural about it: it was magical in nature. I could see the matrix of the spell flickering amongst the green-tinted flames. I'd never seen anything like it. Magic could be used to start a fire, just like a match or flint and tinder. It was about generating that first spark. This was something else entirely, and it distracted me until I heard a throat clear and tore my eyes away in search of the woman we'd come to see.

The only other person in the room besides myself and John was a young woman who didn't even look old enough to drink. Legally, anyway. She was sitting at a desk with two computer monitors on it but had swiveled in her plush desk chair to look over at us as we entered. She wasn't even Indian, which surprised me. I was sure we were still on Pueblo lands, and they're strict about who they allow to settle in their territory. The left side of her face was an unattractive mass of scar tissue that crept up into her red hair, but her blue eyes were clear and friendly.

"Kassidy," John said. "This is the woman I told you about."

"Emily Davenport." Kassidy studied me with open curiosity. "Of the Davenport coven, yes? From Boston?" She had a very formal way of speaking, and her voice bore a soft Irish lilt.

If I stared, it didn't have anything to do with the fact that she'd had half her face melted at some point or that she was living in the middle of nowhere with mysterious magic fire and a dual 32-inch monitor setup that'd make Matt squee. It was the fact that—as far as I could tell—she didn't have a lick of magic in her that threw me for a loop.

"Yes," I said belatedly. "I mean, sort of. It's a long story."

"Well, I've got time." She smiled. "John, why don't you take Emily's coat and make us some tea? You do like tea, don't you Emily?"

"Yes," I answered, reaching up automatically to unbutton my coat and letting John slip it from my shoulders. I didn't even pay attention to what he did with it afterward. He could've fed it to the magic flames, and I wouldn't have noticed. Absently, I pulled off my hat and stuffed my gloves in it so I wouldn't lose them. I held on to those, drifting a little farther into the room. "You're... not what I expected."

"Thanks," the other woman said, with an impish gleam in her bright blue eyes. "Have a seat. I know you have questions."

I did. So many, in fact, that I wasn't sure quite where to start.

CHAPTER 25

I ended up perched at one end of the blue plaid sofa, my hat and gloves resting in my lap. I forced myself to lean back, not wanting to seem too eager.

Just play it cool, Em.

"So, uh, where do we start?" I asked, leaning an elbow on the arm of the sofa.

"Well, we could start with the usual questions. Who am I, how did I end up here, and what makes John think I can help you?" Kassidy replied.

I couldn't help but smile. This was a woman after my own heart. Straight to the point. I respected that. "That sounds about right to me. But, uh, does John bring you strays often?" My eyes slid toward the man in the kitchen, but there was no reaction. Either he was tuning us out or at least giving the illusion that he was.

Kassidy chuckled. "Not often. But before we begin, I should tell you... I'm a very private person, and I don't welcome unwanted attention. If I am to help you, I must have your assurance that you won't reveal anything you may learn about me to anyone else. Whatever I'm able to tell you about your own abilities, those morsels are yours to hoard or share as you see fit. But when it comes to me... I do not exist. I don't want to seem boorish, but I can make life very uncomfortable for people who cross me."

The sound of John making tea was a mundane backdrop for a very serious opener to our conversation. I raised a brow at what Kassidy had said. There was an unmistakable note of seriousness to her tone. She definitely wasn't joking.

"Okay," I said, deciding that caution was the order of the day. "But if that's how it's going to be, I want the same from you. When it comes to me, my abilities, whatever is going on with me. I don't want you to talk about it with anyone else either."

She smiled. "Fair is fair. What about John?" She inclined her head in the direction of the man leaning against the kitchen counter, looking out the window while he waited for the water to boil. There was no way he was not listening.

"You can talk about it with John. The cat's already out of that particular bag," I said. I'd just have to have a private chat with John when all this was done, to make sure *he* would keep my counsel. I suspected, given his apparent association with Kassidy and her own proclivities when it came to privacy, that he wouldn't have a problem with that. Thinking about it, he had been pretty cagey and non-specific about who it was he wanted to introduce me to.

"Splendid." Kassidy clapped her hands together before folding them across her stomach. Her elbows were resting comfortably on the arms of her chair. "My name, as you know, is Kassidy. You can think of me as an occult librarian. I've spent my entire life studying magic. I maintain a vast archive of information, some of it my own notes, some of it notes and texts written by others. I won't pretend to know everything. I have plenty of texts in my collection that I simply don't understand. But it keeps life interesting, I suppose."

I took all this in quietly, absently fingering the cuff of my knitted hat. "No offense, but you don't look old enough to have very vast experience."

She laughed lightly, eyes twinkling. "Appearances can be deceiving."

The kettle whistled, forestalling my answer momentarily. I was probably squinting unattractively, peering at her for some hint of a spell, a charm, anything that would explain the fact that she looked like an eighteen-year-old girl. Her mannerisms were a little off for someone that age, but otherwise... I wasn't sure what to think.

"Are you affiliated with the Circle?" I asked once John had removed the kettle from the stove, quieting it.

The smooth half of her face screwed up in a scowl. "That presumptuous bunch of self-important feckers? No."

My jaw dropped, but I quickly snapped it shut. Sure, few outside the Circle's allied covens appreciated their meddling in everyone else's business, but I'd never heard anyone speak quite so openly against them. Most were too busy trying not to attract their attention. Before witches went mainstream, the Circle was really good at making the ones who attracted too much attention disappear. These days, their focus had shifted more to PR and image management for witchkind, but they were still a force to be reckoned with.

"Right," I said, more than willing to drop the subject. "Okay, so, what can you tell me about what happened to me?"

Kassidy's scowl faded as swiftly as it came. She leaned

forward slightly in her chair. "I know what John told me about the incident, but secondary sources are always more suspect than primary ones. Why don't you tell me what happened, in your own words?"

"Well, I saw this witch using too much magic. It was like it was being drawn out of him in this long rope, stretching up into the sky. He was just... checked out, you know? Like he was in some sort of trance. I knew he was going to burn out if I didn't do something, so I grabbed him and then I felt his power flowing into me—through me—into the ground. I told Esc— It was like being a magical lightning rod. That's the best explanation I can think of. Anyway, he's okay. The witch. He didn't burn out, and now I have no idea what I did or if I can do it again."

"Fascinating," Kassidy said, after listening quite raptly. "Have you tried? Doing it again."

I shook my head quickly. "No. Honestly, it scared the crap out of me. You see, I can't actually use magic. Whatever spark it is that witches are born with, I've never had it. My whole family has it, but not me."

"Mmhmm. Well, it sounds more like the magic is using you than the other way around." She paused to look up as John brought her a mug of tea and a little caddie with milk and sugar. "Thank you, John."

"So, you've never heard of anything like this?" I asked. Dismay gnawed at the pit of my stomach, like a dog worrying a bone. John brought me a cup of tea too, and I accepted it distractedly, leaning over to set it on the coffee table to cool.

"I never said that," Kassidy said. "But I need to consult the archive. John, do you mind if Emily tries to use her power on you?"

"No, I don't mind," he said without a hint of hesitation.

"Um, what if I mind?" My voice pitched higher than usual thanks to rising anxiety.

"You don't have anything to fear," Kassidy said, smiling at me. The unmelted side of her mouth curved much more naturally than the other. I wondered, idly, how far down the burns went under her T-shirt. "John, stand there in the center of the room where I can have a good look. Just open yourself up, let the magic flow into you."

John set his cup of tea down on the coffee table near mine and walked over to stand where Kassidy had indicated. He'd removed his coat as well, revealing a flannel shirt beneath. While I sat there trying to figure out how I could get out of this, he rolled up his sleeves a few turns, revealing brown forearms up to the elbow. I glimpsed a tribal sun tattoo on his inner arm. Glancing at me, he made a "come here" motion with his head.

Despite my better judgment, I got to my feet and walked over to stand in front of him. "Are you sure about this? I don't want to hurt you."

He smiled down at me. "I'll be fine," he said with way more confidence than I personally had. The telltale glow started to rise around him as he indeed opened himself up, tapping into that innate power of his and letting it flow.

I was momentarily paralyzed. I didn't know what to do, if I should take his face between my hands the way I had with Gabriel, or if I needed to touch him at all. He solved the dilemma by reaching for my hands, wrapping his fingers around mine. His hands were warm and work-roughened. It was awkward, standing there holding hands with this admittedly good-looking man I barely knew. Maybe my discomfort played a role in my ability's failure to manifest.

"More, John." Kassidy spoke from behind me.

I frowned as the glowing nimbus around John pulsed brighter. Hot damn, the man could hold an impressive amount of energy. More than I'd seen Hector use, even. What I'd seen of John's ability when he had placed the binding on Gabriel had barely scratched the surface.

His hands loosened their grip on mine. I thought he was letting go, so I started to drop my hands away, but he slid his hands up to lightly grip my forearms, leaving little else for me to do but grip his in return. I was standing very close to him now, our bodies almost touching, and I closed my eyes, trying to find that piece of myself that had lashed out. I started to feel that prickling tingle against my palms, but try as I might, I couldn't seem to do anything with it. I tried as hard as I could to draw his power into me, to tap into it somehow, but it just wasn't happening.

"I'm sorry," I said, opening my eyes to look up at him. Damn these sensible shoes, I actually had to look *up*. "I don't think this is working."

"You're trying too hard," he said. "Don't think. Just do it."

The magic flared around him again, even brighter. The whites of his eyes started to glow and all I could think about was that he had to be nearing his limit. Was I imagining it or was he starting to tremble a little bit? Surely this witch wasn't dumb enough to burn himself out trying to push me into reacting?

I tried to break contact, but his hands firmed their grip on my arms, refusing to let go. Suddenly, as if something had triggered in my brain, I felt the magic rush in, washing over me much faster than it had with Gabriel. I felt it flow through my body as if I were some sort of pipe for it to push through, finding its way into the ground at my feet. Or, rather, into the floorboards at my feet.

It felt like an eternity, but it couldn't have been more than a few seconds before John shut off the faucet, as it were. The light around him winked out, and as the last of it flowed through me my knees buckled. He caught me as I pitched toward him, arms wrapping securely around my waist to hold me against his chest.

"Good job," he said.

"Very good job," Kassidy agreed, and I heard the sound of keys on the keyboard clicking rapidly behind me.

Closing my eyes, I drew a shaky breath, breathing in the smell of fabric softener and spicy cologne. "I'm okay," I said, pushing away. John let go, but when I wavered a bit he gently grabbed my elbow and steered me toward the couch to sit again. The steaming cup of tea was pressed into my hand before he sat down beside me.

I frowned. "What the hell... I didn't feel this way last time."

"You siphoned a lot more energy this time," John answered, with no attempt at self-aggrandizement. Just stating the facts.

"I guess there's that." I rubbed my face with one hand, looking over at Kassidy, who was typing away rather furiously. "Any ideas?" She didn't answer.

"She might be a while," John said, offering me a knowing smile. "It's a process."

He wasn't wrong. I had finished my cup of tea and started drinking John's by the time Kassidy surfaced again, swiveling in her chair with a satisfied smile on her face. On the upside, I was feeling much stronger. On the downside, I was getting impatient. I looked at her, then at John who just shrugged and looked over at her again. I followed suit.

"Well?" I said, voicing the sentiment we were both clearly feeling.

"You're a Conduit."

"A what?" I said, frowning as I rested the bottom of the warm mug against my leg.

"A Conduit. It's very rare, almost unheard of in this day and age. That's why it gave me so much trouble. Anyway, that's your power."

"Okay... So, I'm a Conduit. What exactly does that mean, for me?"

"Well, the lore is a little sketchy," she said with an unbecoming grimace that twisted the melty side of her face grotesquely. Finally reaching for her own cup of tea that she'd all but ignored this whole time, she sipped it before continuing. "But, from what I could glean, it's kind of like an arcane straw. You don't have the capacity to hold magic on your own, but it can pass through you as you have experienced."

I frowned. "If that's the case, why hasn't it happened before? I grew up in a house full of witches. There was magic all over the place. Why didn't it pass through me then?"

"I don't know. But based on what I just saw, it's not a casual action. There has to be some sort of intent behind it. The first time it happened, it was instinctual. When you tried to force it, it was harder. If you practice, you'll get better at it," Kassidy explained, patiently.

"But what's the point? So, I can suck magic out of witches. If I can't do anything with it, what's the point?

Beside me, John spoke up. "Well, you can suck at either end of a straw…"

Kassidy grinned and touched a pale fingertip to her nose. I looked between them uncomprehendingly for a moment but did eventually catch up. When I did, the implications hit me like a ton of bricks, too. "It can go both ways. I can draw magic out of a witch, or they can draw more magic *through* me."

"Quite possibly. But this is all theoretical. I can do some more research, and we'll need to do more experimentation," Kassidy said.

Frankly, I was all experimented out for one day.

CHAPTER 26

We didn't talk much on the way back to John's house. The walk hadn't gotten any longer, really, but it felt like it with nothing to pass the time but my own thoughts. I'd certainly walked out of my meeting with Kassidy with some valuable information, but I wasn't entirely sure what to make of it. It raised more questions than it answered, really. She seemed committed to helping me figure it out, but I knew that to her I was nothing more than a puzzle. A very intriguing puzzle that would expand her ever-growing archive. I still had a lot of questions about *her* too, none of which had really been answered. Maybe next time.

The hike took about thirty minutes. We had just rounded the last bend in the road when I saw someone up ahead of us. It was difficult to tell if this someone was male or female from a distance, and with the long black hair, it really could have gone either way. Whoever it was, they weren't walking toward us or away from us, just kind of loitering in the road. The more I watched, the more they seemed to be aimlessly meandering. As we got closer, I began to perceive more details.

"Is it just me," I asked eventually, "or is that a crazy person roaming around in the freezing cold without a coat?"

"That does seem to be a crazy person roaming around in the freezing cold without a coat," John answered, a frown etched on his face as he picked up the pace, half-jogging his way up the road to reach the person that much more quickly. I followed suit, keeping pace easily. Sensible shoes, see?

As we drew nearer, the coatless stranger turned toward us, but the motion seemed more absent than out of any awareness that we were there. His dark eyes had a glazed-over quality to them, like someone who was totally high on something or other, and they remained out of focus as he lifted a hand and drummed his fingers against his head. He couldn't have been much more than eighteen.

"Luke? What are you doing out here?" John asked, unzipping his own coat and shrugging it off. "Here, put this on." But there wasn't so much of Luke putting the coat on as there was John putting the coat on Luke. He rubbed the boy's arms and frowned down at his bare, muddy feet. Looking over at me, John flashed me an apologetic look. "I'm sorry to cut our visit short, but I need to take care of this."

"No problem. I understand. You know him? Is he... high?"

"His mother lives up the road. I'll make sure he gets home. He, uh, hasn't been himself since..."

My eyes widened. "He burned out?"

John peered at me. "How did you know that? Can you tell?"

I grimaced and shook my head. "Not exactly. But I think I should help you get him home. Do you know how he burned out?"

John shook his head, curling an arm around the youth's waist and starting to steer him toward his truck. "No, I only heard that it happened. It's terrible when it happens, but even more so to someone so young."

I stepped up on Luke's other side to help John with him. Together, we got him up and into John's truck, where he sat passively sandwiched between me and John all the way up the road to the house a quarter-mile away where Luke's family lived. It was no more remarkable than the others I'd passed on the way in, just another brown adobe dwelling circled by a chain-link fence. The gate was standing open, swinging in the breeze. John honked twice as we pulled up, alerting the house of our arrival. By the time we piled out of the truck, an older woman had come out onto the narrow porch and, seeing Luke with us, came running out to meet us. She had streaks of gray in her black hair, which was twisted back in a severe bun, and a hastily thrown-on shawl hung around her shoulders. Like John, she had that telltale spark marking her as a witch. A few more witches came outside after her, ranging from teenagers to adults, but they hung back rather than crossing the yard.

There was a brief exchange between John and the woman in a language I didn't understand, but I could read enough from their body language to get the gist of it. The older woman was obviously distressed that we'd found Luke wandering around outside with no coat and shoes on and started to herd him off in the direction of the house after thanking John profusely for bringing him home. I might as well have been a tree, for all the notice she paid me.

"Wait!" I called, sensing my window was rapidly closing. John was already turning back toward the truck.

The woman paused, still pushing Luke forward as she looked back at me. "I must get him inside."

"Er, right. I know..." I said, stammering as I moved forward. I sensed, more than saw, John turn back and follow me. "I mean, can I ask you a few questions, once Luke is inside warming up?"

She eyed me suspiciously, but gave a curt nod and said, "Wait here."

As she moved off with Luke, John leaned a little toward me and asked, "What was that all about?"

"The attack the other night, that witch wasn't the first one targeted. What if the same thing happened to Luke?" It sounded a little more far-fetched now that I'd said it aloud than it had in my head. But I was starting to see every burned-out witch as a potential victim.

"That would be... unfortunate," John said, choosing his words carefully. "Come on." He started forward, a hand at my back gently pushing me to come with him.

I dug my heels in, brushing him off. "She said to wait," I protested. "I don't want to be rude. She might know something important and doesn't even know it."

John paused, turning back toward me and offering a hand. His eyes met mine. "Trust me."

I nodded, placed my hand in his, and walked with him to the porch, where the others who had come outside had already gone back in. No sense in standing around in the cold when you don't have to, right? We went up the steps into the house. John closed the door, then stood there just inside, keeping our filthy shoes on the rug so as to not track ice and mud onto the carpet. I felt more than a little self-conscious as I glanced around the living room, its shabby but spotlessly clean interior speaking volumes about the family that lived there. The television was on, and those who had gone back inside were settling around the room either on the couch, the floor, or at the dining table where a card game had clearly been interrupted by our arrival.

No one spoke to us, or even acknowledged we'd entered until the matronly woman returned from settling Luke somewhere or another. She eyed us upon finding us inside rather than outside where we'd been bidden wait, her eyes dropping briefly before she flashed me a look of obvious disapproval. I hadn't realized I was still holding John's hand until then. I let go and stuffed my hand in my pocket, clearing my throat.

"I'm—" I began, but got no farther.

"Marie, this is Emily Davenport. She'd like to ask some questions about Luke. May we come in?" John was polite, formal. It seemed to soothe the woman's ruffled feathers a bit, because she gave her shawl a twitch and nodded before snapping something quietly in that language I didn't understand, brown eyes flashing toward the couch as she spoke. The youngest youth lounging there climbed to his feet and headed off down the hallway Marie had come from, while she headed for the kitchen.

We joined her after taking off our shoes, leaving them with the others inside the door. There's something awkward about being barefoot in a stranger's house. It's like making yourself at home prematurely, you know? And it's not like Marie had rolled out the red carpet and welcomed us with open arms. By the time we joined her she had gone back to work, rolling tamales in the kitchen. A kitchen which smelled heavenly, by the way. If I were a less polite person I would have considered inviting myself to dinner.

While John leaned against the counter like he belonged there, I headed over to the little table where Marie was working and pulled out a chair, settling into it. She glanced up at me briefly but didn't initiate conversation. That left it to me.

"I wanted to ask about the circumstances around Luke's... accident. What happened?" Might as well get to the point.

She didn't answer right away. I could tell from her posture, the way she kept her eyes down, kept resolutely filling the corn husks and rolling them with measured, deliberate movements, that it was a difficult topic. Finally, she looked up again, glancing over at John before settling her dark brown eyes upon me.

"He is a teenager, that's what happened," she said, her tone frank.

"Could you be more, uh, specific? Did you see what happened?"

"No, I was not there. I would have stopped him." She was getting a little defensive, which was not my intention.

"Of course, I didn't mean to imply..." I winced. Really, I didn't have the sort of interview technique that Escobar did. "Did anyone witness it? Where did it happen?"

"At the Thirsty Coyote. He was playing cards, probably cheating. There was a fight and by the end he was... like that."

Unfamiliar with the Thirsty Coyote, I glanced over at John and lifted a brow. He inclined his head and took out a cell phone, fiddling with it while I turned my attention back to Marie. "When was this?"

"Two weeks ago."

"Exactly?"

The woman paused, thinking for a moment. "Yes. Fourteen days, exactly."

I did some quick mental math. It would have been a day after Christina, and with William and Tori also being within forty-eight hours of one another... it very well could be related. I could hear John speaking on the other side of the kitchen, into his phone. His voice was low enough that I couldn't really make it out though.

"Do you know anyone who was there that night? Were any of them... gifted, like your family?"

Her hands stilled, and she looked across the table at me again with acute perception. "Why do you have so many questions about this?" She hadn't answered the question, and I wondered why.

However, she'd asked a good question in return, and I wasn't sure how to answer it. I hesitated a moment before giving her pretty much the same line Escobar had given me. "Because I'd like to make sure it doesn't happen to someone else." It was no less true for being recycled.

Marie watched me for a few long seconds, those dark eyes weighing and measuring before she seemed to reach some decision, nodding to herself. "His girlfriend, Joanna Strand. She has been... not quite right in the head since it happened. Claims that a giant snake climbed out of his mouth and slithered off with Luke's magic in its belly."

It was a stomach-churning image but actually bore some resemblance—in my mind at least— to the magical rope I had seen over Gabriel. It wasn't coming out of his mouth, but it was kind of serpentine, and if the girl had become unhinged... she could be describing what I had seen.

Marie wasn't able to give me any more information, but she did press a dozen tamales wrapped in foil into my hands before she let us go. I held them in the crook of my arm as we made our way back to the truck, filling John in on what he'd missed while he was on the phone.

"That's very interesting," he said, nodding thoughtfully.

"The Thirsty Coyote is closed today, but I know where Joanna Strand's family lives if you want to pay them a visit."

I thought about it while we climbed into the truck, balancing the tamales on my leg while I fastened my seat belt.

The truck's engine roared to life, but John let it idle, looking over at me, patiently waiting.

"We still don't have any evidence that ties Luke to the others," I said, "aside from the second-hand ravings of a theoretically insane girlfriend. But today's probably not a good—"

A sudden knock on my window caused me to jump nearly out of my skin. My head whipped around, looking over to see one of the youths from the house standing beside the truck, waving a hand at me.

I rolled down the window, and he handed me a dirty envelope.

"The night Luke burned out, he had this," he said. "I don't know where he got it, but I hid it because I knew it wasn't his, and Mom would be pissed. Seemed like he'd been through enough, you know? Anyway... I don't want it. It's bad luck." He turned and walked away before I could get a word in edgewise.

"Uh, thanks!" I called after him. Curiosity getting the better of me, I opened the envelope before rolling up the window. Inside was seven hundred twenty-two dollars and sixteen cents.

CHAPTER 27

"Are you sure you don't want some of these tamales?" It had been a quiet, thoughtful trip back down the road to John's house, where we climbed out of the truck but lingered outside behind the vehicles. Luke's mysterious cash was stashed in my coat pocket, and his mother's tamales were tucked in the crook of my arm.

John smiled and shook his head. "No thanks, but Marie makes good tamales. I think you'll enjoy them. If there's anything else I can do to help, let me know."

I nodded, fishing my keys out of my pocket and giving them a toss in my hand, listening to them jingle. "Thanks for your help. I really appreciate it. Maybe it goes without saying, but our meeting with Kass and my powers... That's between us, right?"

He nodded, his expression earnest. "Of course. Call me if you'd like to see her again. I know she can be... intense."

The offer reminded me of the strange Irish woman's intimation that I wasn't the first needful person John had brought her. "What did you mean when you said that running into burning buildings was kind of your thing?"

There was a brief blink. It was clearly not a question he was expecting, but he laughed a moment later, displaying even white teeth as he grinned. "I'm a firefighter."

There were so many jokes to be made there, I just couldn't make up my mind. All of them were very inappropriate, considering I barely knew the man. In the end, I laughed along with him and then said goodbye.

On the way back to town, I dialed Escobar. Hands-free, of course.

I received a suspiciously formal answer. "Escobar."

"Hey, it's Emily. Is this a bad time?"

"Go ahead."

"I think we've got another victim. Er, not fresh, but from the day after Christina."

"Who?"

"His name is Luke. Shit, I didn't get a last name. Sorry. I can get it. But there's a witness who may or may not be crazy, and the kid had a suspicious amount of cash on him when it happened. May or may not be related."

"Okay, sounds good. I'll come by and you can brief me."

"Er, I'm not home..."

"See you soon."

He hung up before I could say anything else, and when the phone rang again almost immediately I didn't even check the caller ID before I picked up. "You really need to work on your people skills."

"Emily? Emily! Help!" The voice on the other end was hushed but frantic.

"Dan?" I glanced at my phone to be sure.

"He's here! He's at the door!"

"Already? I just got off the phone with him..."

"You invited him over? What the fuck!"

"Wait, who is at the door?" I was starting to get the feeling that we weren't talking about the same person.

"Joseph!" he exclaimed. Yup, definitely not talking about the same person.

"Oh. Well, pretend you're not there."

"I already answered the door. He knows I'm here." The words were punctuated by a pounding on said door that was loud enough that I could hear it through the phone.

"Call the cops?"

"That's not going to make him any less pissed. Are you almost home?"

I rubbed my temples. "No, I'm twenty minutes out, minimum. Ask what he wants."

I heard Dan shout it through the door. There was a reply, but it was indistinct over the phone. I thought Dan might repeat it for me, but instead he shouted back, "I don't know what you're talking about, go away!"

There was more pounding, and then I heard Dan shout shrilly, "I'm calling the cops!" If he didn't, the old lady downstairs might. By the time Dan got his own place, I was going to have to move.

"Dan, Escobar is on his way over. Just hang tight and one of us will be there soon. Okay? Don't open the door. Call the cops if you don't feel safe."

By the time I got there, Escobar's car was in the parking lot, and there wasn't anyone in cuffs on the stairs, so I took that as a good sign. I parked and hurried upstairs, where I had to knock to be let in since the keyless deadbolt had been thrown. Inside, Dan and Escobar were waiting.

"Where'd Joseph go?" I asked, awkwardly juggling the wrapped tamales as I shed my coat.

"He took off. I guess he didn't want to get arrested," Dan said, eyeing my package. So to speak. "What's that?"

"Tamales. Hungry?"

After I threw the tamales into the oven, we convened at the table to go over what I'd learned today and how that might fit into the case. While we talked, I opened up the case files that Escobar had brought with him and went through them again. Something was nagging me about them, but I couldn't put my finger on it.

"If Luke really was one of our victims, we have a big problem on our hands," Escobar said. I grimaced and nodded.

Dan gave us both a clueless look. "Why?"

"Because the Thirsty Coyote is on Pueblo lands. It's outside my jurisdiction," Escobar said.

I sighed, knowing full well how difficult tribal police could be to deal with.

"So, you'll have to work with who? That Payne guy?" Dan asked, glancing between us.

This time I answered. "No, even worse. The tribal police."

Escobar rubbed his face, clearly not looking forward to this. "Not just that, but because of the serial nature of the crime, the FBI is probably going to want to get involved."

Even Dan knew enough to groan about that. He was fiddling with a paper clip from one of the files, bending it into a springy shape to play with. "So, we can just not report it, right? Until we know for sure they're related?"

I sighed. "They're related. Even second-hand, Joanna's testimony is pretty telling."

"A giant snake?" Dan said, clearly skeptical.

"She's been traumatized, Daniel."

"Well," Escobar interjected before we could settle into a proper argument. "I'm bound by regulations to notify the tribal police. They probably don't even have an inkling that the kid's attack was an attack. If it was."

My head was starting to swim, and I pressed my thumb and fingertips to my temples as if it might keep my brain from moving around too much. "Well, maybe if we talk to the girlfriend, we can get a direction out of her that the snake —I mean the magic—went. We know what direction it was headed during Gabriel's attack, and we know where William and Tori were attacked—or at least an approximation. They couldn't have gotten far from where they were found."

"Yeah, but you can't triangulate magic like you can a cell signal," Dan said, always willing to rain on my parade.

"I know, but even a general direction could be helpful."

"Assuming they're always in the same place when they're casting the spell."

We went back and forth a bit longer until Escobar cleared his throat to get our attention. Poor guy, he deserved a ref's whistle for Christmas. Maybe a canonization for saintly patience. "I think we're getting a little off-track."

With a shrug and a tiny scowl, I went back to looking through the file folder, paging through bank records, looking for any out-of-the-ordinary transactions. There weren't any. The kitchen timer's shrill beep came as a relief, and I flipped the folder closed with a sigh before going to retrieve our dinner from the oven.

"So, what did Joseph want?" I asked, grabbing a potholder and opening the oven.

"He thinks I took some money from Christina."

"Did you?"

"God! Of course not! I didn't even know she was missing any." Dan huffed, apparently both outraged and morally offended. I glanced over at him in time to see the mangled paper clip launch and sail across the table in my direction, but it fell short, landing on the kitchen tile with a quiet tinkle. Barrington ran over to investigate.

"Emily, didn't you say the kid on the Pueblo had a mysterious lump of cash?" Escobar asked.

"Yeah, but that would be awfully coincidental, wouldn't it? If he just happened to steal the money and then got targeted with the same magic-stealing spell? And just because they're both Indians doesn't mean they know each other." I turned off the oven and gingerly opened the foil wrapping, trying to avoid getting burned by the steam that poured out.

Dan straightened in his seat. "Unless the cash actually has something to do with it."

When I turned to grab paper plates from a drawer, I saw him move in the direction of the front door, and when I came out of the kitchen with the tamales, paper plates, and plastic cutlery, he was rooting through my coat pockets.

"Left side," I offered helpfully, setting everything down on the table while Dan located the dirty envelope and brought it over. Ignoring the food, he dumped it out on the table in a shower of cash, some of the change hitting at just the right angle to go rolling until it fetched up against something else littering the table.

Escobar ignored the food, though he accepted a plate and fork with an automatic murmur of thanks. He was watching Dan, lips pressed together and forehead wrinkled. "That's evidence, be careful."

Dan was not being careful. Once he'd dumped out the cash, pawed through it, staring at it intently before proceeding to pick it up one bill or coin at a time for closer inspection. Escobar reached over and carefully plucked the envelope out of the way, barely touching the edges of it.

Fingerprinting cash is an exercise in futility, but the envelope might prove useful.

"What am I missing?" Escobar asked me, close to frowning by this point. He didn't like being left in the dark.

I could empathize. I had no more clue what Dan was up to than he did and spread my hands helplessly.

"Witches need foci for remote spellcasting," Dan said. "If the money does link Luke and Christina, one of the bills or coins could be spelled."

"I didn't notice any lingering magic when I counted it," I said.

"No offense, sis, but I trust my eyes more than yours."

Offense definitely taken. I crossed my arms. "Luke and Christina burned out almost two weeks ago. Even I know a focus spell wouldn't last that long without maintenance."

When it became clear that Dan wasn't about to give up until he'd thoroughly and obsessively inspected every piece of currency littering the table, I served myself a couple of tamales and started eating without him. Escobar followed suit, murmuring in approval at the first taste. I agreed with him. Marie's tamales were excellent.

"Yeah, there's nothing here," Dan said after a few minutes. He shoved the money back into the envelope and grabbed some food for himself.

I didn't even say I told you so.

About halfway through my second tamale, my eyes fell on the folder of bank statements I'd pushed aside minutes earlier. A few of them were sticking out haphazardly, all with the stylized southwestern logo of Del Norte Credit Union.

Reaching out, I flipped open the folder and sifted through the statements with one hand, still holding my fork with the other. "Did you notice that all of the victims had accounts at Del Norte?" I said, glancing over at Escobar.

He nodded. "Yeah. So does half of Santa Fe. We didn't find anything odd in their records."

"What about Gabriel? Didn't he mention going to the bank the day of the attack?" I didn't see a statement for him in the file.

Escobar took out his notepad and flipped through it, brow furrowing. "He did, but he didn't say which one."

I pushed my plate away in favor of the bank records again, once more getting that nagging feeling that there was something there. I grabbed a pen from the table and uncapped it with my teeth, keeping the cap between my teeth while I started circling dates. The pen cap fell out a few moments later, hitting the edge of the table and careening off onto the floor.

"That's it!" I pushed my plate farther away and spread the pages out in front of me, using the pen as a pointer. "Look here. Christina. Check cashed. Tori. Deposit and withdrawal. Same amount, probably just making change. William. Withdrawal." Tearing my eyes away from the emerging evidence in front of me, I looked between Dan and Escobar. "Within twenty-four hours of their attacks, they all went to the bank. Every single one. And not just that, but they all walked out with cash in hand."

CHAPTER 28

"This is a waste of time," Dan complained. It was getting late, and we were deep in the bowels of the police station, going through a box of evidence bags in search of any cold hard cash William or Tori might have had on them when they were attacked.

"You wanted to help," I reminded him, pulling one at a time out, reading or observing its contents and setting it aside. Not even our pretty consultant badges had gotten us in here; Escobar had to sign out the evidence to preserve chain of custody. Technically, he probably shouldn't have left us alone with it, but he had to go wake up a bank manager to try and get more information about the transactions that had been made at the credit union. If they were all processed by the same teller, well, we'd be on even steadier ground.

"Yeah, but this is still a waste of time. There no way I can sniff out a spell that old, even if I did have use of my magic."

I rolled my eyes. "You were pretty intent on inspecting Luke's ill-gotten gains," I pointed out, finding a bag from Tori's box with a few coins in it and passing it to Dan so he could inspect it more closely. I trusted his eyes better than mine right now, running on about five hours of sleep and liberal caffeine consumption.

"Wishful thinking, I guess. Besides, I didn't realize the trail was two weeks old when I started." He started to open the bag.

"Don't do that!" I said, reaching out to snatch the bag from his hands. Or try, anyway. He was fast, yanking it up out of my reach like Lucy with Charlie Brown's football. I glared at him. "Leave it in the bag. Escobar said not to touch anything."

He smirked, holding up the bag and peering at the change inside but making no further attempt to open it. "I don't see anything, but if there's some sort of residue I might be able to sense it by touch."

"I thought this was a waste of time?"

"Blow me."

"In your lonely, pathetic, incestuous dreams."

He tossed the bag on the table with another smirk, watching while I went through the second box. "It's that Gabriel guy we should be checking out. If he's got a spell focus, it's only a couple days old. Probably still has some juice."

"We'll go bother him when we're done here. Escobar had to get the ball rolling with the bank manager first."

"We could have taken two cars," he said, folding his arms.

Pausing, I glanced over at him with a frown. "It was quicker to ride with Escobar."

"You just wanted to ride in the car with the flashy lights."

My cheeks heated. He wasn't entirely wrong, but I didn't give him the satisfaction of answering. Instead, I turned my attention back to the box.

My silence and slight flush was all the confirmation he needed. He leaned against the table and asked, "Did you like the siren too? Woowoowoo!"

"Shut up."

"Do you want to ride in the back on the way to the motel? Maybe the detective would put some handcuffs on you if you asked nicely. Or— maybe you two would like to be alone?" He honest-to-goodness waggled his brows at me. I threw a plastic R2D2 keychain in an evidence bag at him. He snickered but relented. "Are you going to tell me about your visit with what's his name's old Indian woman?"

"His name's John, and she wasn't old or an Indian. Just a woman. We can talk about it later," I said, a bit too distracted by my search to realize I was already saying too much.

"Was she hot?"

I ignored him, finally locating an evidence bag with money in it from Hines's box. I smacked him in the chest with it, then picked R2D2 up off the floor and tossed it back into the box with the rest. He caught the bag before it fell and dutifully inspected its contents without opening it. "Don't see anything. Not that I expected to."

I grabbed the bag and peered at it myself, but reached the same unfortunate conclusion that Dan had. "Okay, maybe this was a waste of time," I conceded. I don't like to admit I'm wrong, but sometimes it's worthwhile to set a good example.

He didn't gloat, much. But he did grab a chair and spun it around, settling into it and folding his arms across the top of the front-facing chair back. "So, seems like we have plenty of time to talk about John's not-so-old, not-so-Indian woman."

I dropped into a chair, glancing at my phone to check

the time. It was a delaying tactic, but whatever. There was a notification on the screen. Matt had texted me hours ago.

Matt: Why are you ghosting Barry? He's a catch.

Ghosting Barry? Okay, so I hadn't returned his text the day before. Hell, I'd barely given him a second thought amidst the shitstorm that'd become my life over the last forty-eight hours. But he had no way of knowing how crazy it'd been—unless Matt had told him, anyway—and what lay at the heart of the chaos was so deeply personal that I doubted Matt would betray my confidence.

I fired off a quick reply to my well-meaning BFF, then opened my message thread with Barry. His invitation to coffee was still sitting there, waiting for me. Points to Barry for not sending a slew of follow-ups.

Dan cleared his throat, reminding me he was still waiting for my answer. I sent Barry a quick apology and assured him I'd be in touch in a few days when things quieted down, then put my phone away again.

What could I tell Dan about my visit with Kassidy? It had left me with more questions than answers, and if what we'd deduced about my abilities was true, I wasn't sure I wanted to share it with anyone. Not even Dan. Okay, especially not Dan. Plus, she'd basically sworn me to secrecy when it came to things about the visit that didn't directly relate to my abilities. I didn't want to break that confidence, even if I hadn't really learned much about her. She was still a fairly intriguing person.

When I looked up again, Dan was watching me. Really, sometimes he had no concept at all of what is and isn't polite. Or maybe he just didn't care. I could envy that, at times. "There's not much to tell, really. We had tea. We talked. She wanted me to try to demonstrate what I'd done."

His brows lifted. "Did you?"

"Yeah."

"With her?"

For some reason, I was reluctant to answer. But I did anyway. "With John."

His brows went up. Maybe I'd hesitated too long. "Huh. And it worked? Same as before?"

"Yeah. I mean, not immediately. But I got it, eventually. Same as before." I fiddled absently with one of the evidence bags, desperately needing something to do with my hands. I am not a good liar. I hoped it didn't come down to that.

"So, what did she say? Did you get any, I dunno, insight?"

Shit. It was going to come down to that. I shrugged. "She said she'd do some research, and we'd have to do some more experimentation." True. Technically.

He nodded, not seeming to find anything amiss. "Well, I don't know if you can do anything with me because of the... you know. But if you want to try, I'm game."

I nodded, feeling a small twinge of guilt. Very small. The more time I spent with Dan, the more I had to remind myself that I wasn't supposed to like him. He grows on you. Kind of like moss, or a persistent toenail fungus.

By the time we got to the motel, it was almost midnight. Fortunately, Doris wasn't on duty. The fresh-faced uniform that was stationed inside the warded motel room seemed relieved for someone to show up, probably tired of sitting there in the dark while Gabriel slept. It had to be only slightly preferable to sitting outside in a cold car.

As cooperative as Gabriel was when we were there before, he was none too pleased about being woken up so we could root through his belongings. But he did confirm that he was a Del Norte Credit Union member and had cashed his paycheck the day of his attack. Most of it had been dutifully turned over to Mrs. Sanchez, but he did have some of it left over. Walking-around-money, he said as he fished it out of his pants pocket and passed it over to me. I sifted through the change on my way to the door, which had been left open so Dan could watch from outside, behind the shimmering spiderweb of wards that kept him out. I started to get a sinking feeling.

"I think this is a no-go. I should have realized before," I said, stopping just inside the wards.

"What?" Dan asked, eyeing me and the change in my upturned palm.

"The wards. They're supposed to keep magic out. They wouldn't have let a spell focus pass." I closed my fingers into a fist and passed said fist through the wards without difficulty. I dropped the change into Dan's waiting hand.

"Yeah, but were they up when he went in?"

"Good point, but they went through fine just now."

Dan pawed through the change, peering at it intently, then flung it at the wall with a frustrated growl. It scattered, some of it flying into the room and other bits falling to the icy concrete outside. "Goddammit!" He gave the wall a kick for good measure. "It must be a one-shot item."

"Or it wore off before we got Mr. Sanchez to the motel. It took a few hours," Escobar said, behind me.

I turned to look at him, then flashed Gabriel a faint smile. "On the upside, I think you can safely go home now."

He grunted, turning to climb back into the warm bed. "Room's paid up for the night, right?"

CHAPTER 29

The next morning, Dan was nowhere to be found. Neither was my car. One of these things was considerably more inconvenient than the other. I'll leave which to your imagination.

Fortunately, my ask-forgiveness-rather-than-permission brother hadn't run off with my phone again too. I used it to call Escobar, who left me cooling my heels at home with the promise to call me if there were any developments in the case. Normally, I don't mind hanging around my apartment on my day off. I can be kind of a homebody at times. But there's nothing that makes you want to go somewhere quite as much as having no transportation. Suddenly, the coffee didn't taste as good. Nothing I had in the house to eat sounded appetizing. There was nothing on television. Even the internet, my old standby, failed to entertain.

They say that idle hands are the devil's workshop. I may not believe in the devil, nor am I really sure who "they" are, but by mid-morning I was definitely up to no good—or at least up to ill-advised do-gooding. You see, I couldn't help but notice that Del Norte Credit Union was only a short rideshare away, and I might not have had my car but I did have my wallet. Impulse control isn't always my strong suit. Forty-five minutes later, I stood on the curb while the taxi pulled away. My breath frosted in the cold air, and large snowflakes drifted down lazily from the gray sky above.

It didn't occur to me that my reason for being there wasn't a valid business reason until I walked through the front door. If there's one thing banks don't appreciate, it's random people loitering in the lobby. There were a few people in line for the tellers when I got there, and a few more filling out forms on the tall station for such things in the middle of the room. I strode purposefully in that direction, smiling and waving when one of the tellers called out a friendly welcome. I grabbed a deposit slip and a pen, then started pretending to fill the slip out while surreptitiously checking out the tellers.

It was getting on toward lunchtime. Almost every station was open, but I didn't pick up a magical signature from any of the tellers. What did that mean? Maybe the teller had been fired. Maybe they were on break. Maybe they were working the drive-thru. Maybe it was their day off.

Maybe we were still on the wrong track.

I pushed that thought away and doodled a bit more on my deposit slip, debating my next move. I didn't get very far, because a familiar voice spoke behind me.

"How long do you think you can get away with doodling on that deposit slip?" Dan's teasing tone was unmistakable, but at least he was being quiet. I glanced over my shoulder to snark back at him, but there was nothing but air behind me.

Blinking, I looked around before turning back to what I had been doing. Or, at least to the appearance of what I had been doing. Was my mind playing tricks on me?

"Oh man, if you could see the look on your face. It's priceless." The voice came from off to the left this time, still a whisper. I glanced over but saw nothing.

"Are you crazy?" I asked in a tense whisper. "What the hell are you doing?"

"Same thing you're doing, sis. Trying to get a bead on our suspect." He'd moved again. I could practically feel him behind me, a tingle along my back where the invisible spell brushed against me. Why couldn't I see the spell? Who the hell had the alarming lack of foresight to teach Dan, of all people, an invisibility spell? And how on earth was he using magic at all, bound as he was?

"You're using an invisibility spell. Inside a bank. Are you crazy?" I said, going back to trying to look like I was filling out the slip. Frowning, I scribbled on it like I'd made a mistake and ripped it in half, then reached for another. I scanned the room as I did so, locating the usual protective wards around the room. Why wasn't Dan triggering them?

"You're the one standing here apparently talking to yourself, and I'm the one that's crazy?"

He was enjoying this way too much. I glared at him over my shoulder, but it wasn't as satisfying when I couldn't tell if he'd moved again.

"I'm going to see if I can get into the break room." His voice receded as he moved away.

"Dan, no! Wait!" There was no answer.

Well, shit.

Sometimes men are like toddlers, you just have to let them hurt themselves or they won't learn. Unfortunately, I felt kind of responsible for this particular toddler, despite my better judgment. But it was out of my hands for the moment.

I lingered a little longer, then made a show of looking for

something in my wallet before sighing and turning back toward the door. I couldn't justify standing there any longer, no matter how much I may have wanted to. I was turning to go when a tall, well-groomed stranger stepped into my path. His gray polo shirt featured the credit union's logo embroidered on the breast.

He smiled solicitously. "Can I help you?"

I didn't answer, staring at his chest in sudden realization. I'd seen that shirt before. Okay, not that exact shirt, but its twin. The witch from the cafe, the older guy that'd been sitting under that magnificent painting, he'd been wearing it.

"Miss?"

My eyes snapped to the man's face. I fumbled for an adequate cover story. "Sorry. I, uh, can't find my ID. I'll have to come back."

"Did you need to make a withdrawal? You can make a deposit without an ID as long as you know your account number and don't need your balance printed on the receipt." He was so friendly and helpful. I instantly felt bad for my deception, but it really was for the greater good.

"Er, no. I mean, yeah. Sorry. Thanks, though."

He gave me an odd look as I retreated in the direction of the door, heading back outside through the climate-controlled entryway and out into the midday sun. That could have gone better. I glanced over my shoulder through the glass doors, but the man had already moved on to another customer. Hopefully, he didn't spare me another thought.

Unsure what to do next, I sat down on a bench outside to consider my options. Could the witch from the cafe be the one we were looking for? I hadn't seen any other witches in the bank, but that didn't mean he was the only one employed there. I took my phone out and considered calling Escobar, but that'd mean admitting what I'd been up to on my own. And I didn't have enough evidence to point the finger at anyone yet. I put the phone back in my pocket.

My eyes skimmed the parking lot, and I located my car parked on the far edge. If I'd had my keys, I might have taken off and left Dan to find his own way back home. It would have served him right. But I reasoned that once he'd finished scoping the place out he'd come back outside. After about five minutes, I got up and walked over to the car, leaning against the driver's door to wait. Better safe than sorry.

Thirty minutes later, Dan materialized halfway across the parking lot, walking toward me at a steady clip. "Hop in! We've gotta go." He unlocked the door and pushed me bodily aside so he could open it.

"Hey! You've got some nerve, you know."

I didn't get any further, because he grabbed me and shoved me into the open door. I could have resisted if I'd wanted to, but I went along with it, crawling through the car to sit in the passenger's seat while Dan scrambled in behind me and slammed the door closed. The engine rumbled to life while I shot daggers at my brother from my side of the car.

"What the hell, man? Where were you this morning, and how did you—"

He cut me off with an upheld hand and gazed intently out the windshield. A slow grin formed on his face. "Gotcha."

I followed the direction of his gaze, observing the familiar witch from the cafe—wearing his usual credit union polo—as he approached a nearby car from the direction of the building. "Okay, I know what you're thinking, but—"

"He was the only witch in the whole building."

"That doesn't mean he's—"

Dan gunned the accelerator like a race car driver. But he didn't pull out until the witch did, following him out of the parking lot and into midday traffic. I hurriedly put my seat belt on, then busted out my phone to thumb through my contacts.

"What are you doing?" Dan asked.

"Calling Escobar."

He snatched the phone from my hand and, I kid you not, threw it out the window.

"What the fuck?" I twisted in my seat, craning my neck to try and see where it landed. "Seriously?"

"We don't need him," Dan said, changing lanes. "He'll just get in the way."

"We're not cops, Dan! What are we going to do, roll up and declare a citizen's arrest? We don't even know that he's the witch we're looking for."

"If he is, he's dangerous."

"I know, which is why we shouldn't be going in on our own!"

"I can do this. I need to do this." His hands tightened on the wheel, jaw set stubbornly. He looked over at me, a little too long for my taste, considering we were in a moving automobile he was supposed to be driving. "Don't worry. I'll keep you safe."

"You can start by keeping your eyes on the road."

"Sorry." He put his attention back where it belonged. We turned left two blocks later, still in casual pursuit.

I folded my arms, watching the road. "You know, this is basically kidnapping, right?"

"Gonna press charges?" he asked, with a quiet snicker.
"I'm keeping my options open."
"You're cute when you sulk."
"I've got a taser in my purse."
Longest. Ten. Minute. Drive. Ever.

CHAPTER 30

The witch pulled his gold sedan into a driveway on a residential street. It was a nice area, the sort where parents don't worry too much about letting their kids play outside without supervision. Well, at least as much as any modern helicopter parent allows.

The property was circled by a low stone wall with a metal fence sprouting from it, except for the gap where the driveway cut through the yard to the garage. The house beyond was adobe, squat and brown, but featured large windows and several chimneys.

Dan parked on the curb opposite the house. The car had barely stopped before he opened the door and jumped out. He hadn't even turned it off.

"Hey!" I reached over to kill the ignition. "Where are you going?"

"Gotta get inside before he closes the door!" Dan took off across the narrow road. This time I saw the glow of magic around him as he briefly drew on his gift to cast a spell. I even saw the threads of the spell start to come together before they twisted sideways and vanished right along with him. How was he *doing* that? I hadn't even had the presence of mind to ask him how he'd broken his binding while we were driving, much less how he made a spell—and himself—invisible.

"Idiot!" I slammed my palm against the dash in frustration, then leaned over to snatch the keys from the ignition. Throwing open the door—and nearly losing it to a passing car that laid on the horn—I got out and slammed it before stuffing the keys in my pocket and making my way across the street in Dan's wake. By the time I got to the front door, it was long since closed.

"Well, did you make it?" I asked the air, uncertain if my brother was still outside. When I got no answer, I leaned on the doorbell. There's more than one way to skin a cat.

The witch answered the door within seconds. He couldn't have gotten very far into the house before I rang the bell. I put on my most friendly and apologetic smile.

"I'm so sorry to bother you. I just saw you get home and, well, my car won't start. Can I borrow your phone?" I jerked a thumb over my shoulder in the direction of my little Toyota sitting across the street, hoping this guy was as unfamiliar with his neighbors as I was mine.

He hesitated but opened the door wider. "Sure, yeah." He was an older gentleman, clean-cut but with deep lines in his face like he'd spent too long carrying too many burdens. Stepping back, he held the door open for me, and I moved inside. There weren't any wards in the doorway, which struck me as odd. Most witches have some sort of protection spells on their home, fire retardants and the like, but for whatever reason, there was nothing here, not even the tiniest trickle of power.

"Thanks, I really appreciate it." I glanced around but

didn't see any sign of Dan. Or much else, beyond a meticulously tidy living room.

The witch fished his cell phone out of his pocket and offered it to me. "No landline, sorry."

"Who has one of those anymore, right?" I tried to take the phone from him, but he tightened his hold and held on, squinting at me.

"Have we met?"

"No," I answered a little too quickly. "I mean, I don't think so. I, uh, get that a lot. One of those faces I guess."

He didn't appear to be buying my nervous laughter but released his grip on the phone. I stared at it a moment, dumbly. Now what? I didn't know Escobar's number off the top of my head. 9-1-1 seemed premature. So I dialed the only number I knew by heart: Matt's.

He picked up after a few rings. The sound of his voice was more comforting than it should have been, given my current predicament.

"Hi, I need to arrange a tow," I said, turning away so I didn't have to look at the witch directly while I lied through my teeth.

"Em? Is that you? What's going on? Where are you?" He sounded concerned, and rightly so. More rightly than he knew.

"Yeah, it won't start. I'm on, uh," I glanced over my shoulder at the witch. "Sorry, what street are we on?"

"Ocotillo Street. 321."

I turned back and repeated the address for Matt.

"Why don't you just call a service? Is something wrong?" Poor Matt. I was going to owe him big time after this little caper.

"Uh-huh, yeah. Escobar. E-s-c-o-b-a-r. Emily. Just send a

truck. I'll be waiting with the car. Red Toyota. Make it fast, will you? It's freezing out there."

"Em, look out!" I heard Dan's sudden warning from somewhere behind me a moment before pain exploded behind my eyes. Also, in the back of my head. The phone slipped from my fingers as I went down. I hit the carpet and lay there dazed for a moment. I could hear Matt's panicked voice calling out my name through the phone, which lay a few feet away.

Apparently, it's not as easy to knock someone out by hitting them on the back of the head as movies would have us believe. The strike had hurt like hell, though, and dazed me for a few seconds. Say what you will about my little brother, but he wasn't about to stand idly by while some stranger rolled me up in a rug or something. I heard a startled grunt and a noisy thud while I held my head, my concerns about the witch's innocence quickly melting away.

"Matt! Call the cops," I groaned, hoping he'd hear me. I couldn't hear him calling anymore over the rush of blood in my ears and the sounds of crashing in the room. Maybe he was one step ahead and had already hung up. A girl can dream.

When I managed to lift my head to look around, I saw that the orderly room had dissolved into chaos in a remarkably short time. There was a scorch mark on one wall and overturned furniture, coasters, and remotes strewn everywhere. Dan, now visible, had taken refuge behind an armchair, while the couch shielded the older witch. Both glowed brightly as they worked their will, weaving together spell and counterspell, slinging them back and forth like gunslingers firing from cover. An unnatural wind whipped through the room, blowing in my face and raising the hairs on the back of my neck. This was going nowhere fast, and someone was going to get hurt—probably me.

Pushing myself up onto my hands and knees, I swallowed a sudden wave of nausea and crawled for my purse, which had somehow ended up under the coffee table. I had one thought in mind—well, aside from wanting to puke and curl up in a ball, preferably not in the puke—and that was to get the pepper spray out of my purse and end this little stand-off.

A sudden blur of movement drew my eyes from the prize. I looked up in time to see Dan rocket across the room. He vaulted over the couch and bowled the surprised witch over, resorting to fisticuffs to settle the dispute. Dan had the edge, being the younger and fitter of the two. The witch took several solid blows to the face before he managed to get his fingers around my brother's neck. A magical glow sprang to life around him, and I knew Dan was in trouble even before they rolled over with the other witch in the dominant position. Dan had gone completely limp, lying there staring upward as power flared around him and magic began to flow, visibly, from him toward the chest of his assailant.

It was just like the night I'd witnessed Gabriel being attacked, but the magic serpent didn't have a long distance to travel this time. The asshole was sucking out my brother's mojo right in front of my eyes.

"No!" I cried, changing course and scrambling toward them. The witch shifted his grip, keeping one hand on Dan's neck. I didn't see the other one coming. He backhanded me as soon as I got close enough, and I saw stars again, falling on my back on the thin carpet. I knew I didn't have much time, but I'd fallen close enough that I could grab Dan's limp hand and reach out in desperation for that yet-unfamiliar ability the last week's events had stirred. I felt the tingle almost immediately, and Dan's magic started to flow into me. It was like stepping into a cool stream. As it washed over me it brought with it a strange sort of alertness and clarity. I pressed the other hand against the rug, and I could feel the magic spreading across the floor from my fingertips.

It took a moment for the witch to realize what was going on. The flow of magic between him and Dan slowed, even as the glow around Dan grew brighter. Whatever spell he was trying to work, I was stronger. What's more, I was starting to feel stronger, too. I sat up, gripping Dan's hand tightly and wearing a mighty glare. The witch stopped what he was doing, and the glow instantly winked out around Dan as he slipped unconscious like an overindulgent prom date.

Unfortunately, my clarity slipped away as quickly as Dan's magic, the last of it flowing through me and leaving me feeling thick-headed and drained. I didn't have the reflexes to jerk away quickly enough when the witch lunged for me, but I fought him nonetheless. He managed to catch my wrists and pin them against the carpet. Despite my best efforts, I couldn't seem to get a knee placed where it was discouraging enough.

Magic flared around him again, and it felt like a fist plunged into my chest as the spell he'd used on Dan and the others was turned on me. I think I screamed. I'm really not sure. All I know is that there wasn't anything in there for it to grab until, suddenly, there was.

If bleeding off Dan's magic had been like dipping my toes in a cool stream, this was like standing in front of a goddamn fire hose. My vision sharpened as power flowed through me and into the witch, whose eyes widened, their whites glowing as the amount of energy he was channeling suddenly increased dramatically. The glowing aura around him flared brighter too, like a star going supernova.

What was it Suzi had said? Something about a man with silver hair and lightning in his eyes? I vowed to take her dream visions more seriously next time. If I survived for there to be a next time, anyway.

I closed my eyes against the brightness, and the last thing I remember hearing was his laughter.

CHAPTER 31

I woke in an unfamiliar room with an ache in my head and a mouth so dry it felt like a whole colony of dust bunnies had taken up residence while I was out. I was lying somewhere soft, at least. When I groaned and lifted a hand to my head, Dan was suddenly at my side, his concerned face hovering over the edge of the bed.

"Em? Are you okay?" There was no concealing the worry in his voice.

Annoyance flared. He'd gotten me into this mess, after all. "Asshole." I pushed myself up a bit gingerly and scooted back so I could lean against the wall. I was sitting on a twin bed in what looked like more of a spare bedroom than a cell. One works with what one has, I suppose. It was a largely windowless room, with just two squat windows high on one wall, both of which were reinforced with magical wards. All four walls glowed with mystical sigils too, warded against eavesdropping. Or—in our case—to keep anyone from hearing us screaming for help. "How long was I out?"

"Couple of hours." He sat on the edge of the bed. I studied him for a long moment while I took stock of my injuries. My head hurt, my face hurt, and my wrists were a little bruised. Otherwise, I felt okay. Tired. Rode hard and put away wet, Matt might say.

"Damn, I'd expect Matt to have the cavalry here by now."

"It might've been, if he'd given you the right address. I don't know what the house number is, but we're not on Ocotillo Street."

Groaning, I shook my head slowly. "How'd he know I wasn't on the level?"

"Has anyone ever told you you're a terrible liar? Also, I think he recognized you or something."

I eyed him from my end of the bed. "How long were you out?"

He shrugged, raking his fingers through his pale hair. "Forty-five minutes or so."

"So you've been awake long enough to have plenty of time to think about how stupid this was?" I folded my arms, then lifted one hand to pinch the bridge of my nose—which was, incidentally, pretty much the only part of my face that didn't hurt.

Dan smirked, shifting to lean on a hand planted beside him on the bed. "It was a pretty good idea until you decided to party crash."

"Riiight. Sneaking into the bad guy's house by yourself, unarmed, without telling anyone what you were doing…"

"Hey! You knew. You were supposed to be my backup in case something went sideways." He had a point, but I wasn't about to let logic get in my way at that juncture.

"What if I hadn't been at the bank? Then what?" I glared at him pointedly.

He shifted uncomfortably where he sat. "I dunno. But I was just going to take a look around and sneak back out again."

I didn't believe him, but I let it go. For the moment. Sort of. "This is so typical of you. You don't think. You just hare off on whatever whim suits you without a care for how that affects anyone around you."

Dan rolled his eyes, ending up gazing across the room rather than looking at me. "Whatever. Think what you want."

"I know what kind of man you are." I eyed him from my position at the head of the bed. "The sort that won't take responsibility for anything. The sort that walks away from his kid before it's even born."

He tensed but didn't answer. Well, good. He had it coming, and I was going to give it to him.

"How much do you think Mom paid her, to get her to go away? Do you think it's enough to set them up for life? Do you think it'll make up for growing up without a father, wondering what kind of sack of shit just walks away and doesn't give a crap?" My head throbbed harder, probably in response to my rising blood pressure.

Dan kept staring across the room, enduring my verbal onslaught with a stubborn set to his jaw. He didn't answer, so I leaned over and gave his shoulder a shove with one hand.

"I didn't have a choice," he said, still not looking my way. His voice sounded wooden. Hollow. That should've told me something, but I was too fired up to pick up on it.

"Of course you had a choice. There's always a choice." I shoved him again.

He turned his head, finally looking at me again. Our eyes met. What I saw in them gave me pause.

"They didn't give me a choice." His voice was thick with anger. No. Anguish.

"What do you mean?"

"I didn't even know about the baby before it was 'taken care of.' No one asked me what I wanted or gave me the opportunity to do the right thing, alright? So back the fuck off."

He looked away again, pressing the heels of his hands to his eyes while I sat there staring at him with slowly dawning horror, jaw hanging open. It's not that I didn't know my mother was a piece of work, but I hadn't seen that coming. Not by a long shot. I didn't know what to say. What do you say in the face of something like that?

Dan was quiet for a long moment, but his hands fell away to rest on his knees, and he sat there staring at the floor with a haggard expression that looked so foreign on his face.

Pushing off of the wall, I scooted over to sit beside him and wrapped an arm around his waist, then lay my head on his shoulder. "Christ, Dan. Why didn't you just tell me that to start with?"

"I didn't want to talk about it. It was easier to let you think what you wanted to think." He sighed. "But I can't do it anymore. I know I'm not perfect, but I'm not a monster, Em. I swear. If Mom hadn't thrown me out, I would've left anyway. I hate her."

I felt awful, and not just because of my budding concussion and bruised face. He was my little brother, and our mother had treated him even more roughly than she'd ever treated me. What's worse, I could see shades of her in myself and my reactions since his arrival. I wanted to take it all back, but what was done was done.

"I'm sorry." It felt lame, but it was all I had.

"It's okay."

"No, it's not. I'm the worst sister ever."

"Well, to be fair, you haven't had a lot of practice," he

said, shades of the old Dan returning as the vulnerable stranger shrank back into his flippant shell.

Smirking, I squeezed him again before withdrawing to sit once more with my back to the wall. "I'm guessing you're bound again?"

He grimaced, glancing toward the door. "Yeah, must have happened while I was out."

"How'd you get unbound to start with? And how'd you do that invisibility thing? I couldn't even see the spell after you cast it."

He turned his head, looking over at me with a decidedly smug smile. "What, you think you're the only witch in the family with talent?"

"Out with it. You're the only outlet I have for my rage right now, so you'd do well to distract me." Not that I hadn't done a good job of raging all over him already.

"Fine, fine. I can twist spells. Ones that don't require active maintenance, anyway. It turns them invisible."

My eyebrows went up, and it hurt. I winced and dragged the tips of my fingers down my forehead like I might be able to pull them back down again. "That's how you became invisible?"

"No, it's how the invisibility spell became invisible. Normally it'd only fool mundies. I wasn't sure if it'd fool the wards at the bank even after it was twisted, but it did. Pretty cool, right?" He grinned.

"Does Mom know?"

His grin lingered. "No. I figured it out when I was a kid, and it was too much fun to play with when no one knew."

That sounded about right for him. A thought occurred to me. "That's why you were checking out those coins so carefully. You thought maybe he could do it too." He nodded reluctantly. I chuckled in spite of myself but hadn't lost track of the details. "What about the binding?" I paused. "The original one. Mom's."

"Your buddy John took care of that for me."

"John Warren?" There went the eyebrows again. I left them alone this time.

"Yeah. I figured it was a long shot, but I bought him breakfast and explained the situation, and he agreed to do it."

"How'd you even..." I groaned when it hit me. "You used my phone again." A familiar anger was starting to bubble, and I shot him a small glare. "You'd better hope the witch that threw us in here kills you, because if not, I'm going to do it when we get out."

Dan put up his hands in a placating gesture. "Hey, hey, I think you're losing sight of the important thing here."

"Really. What is that?"

"Johnny-boy would totally have breakfast with you on a moment's notice. I think he's sweet on you."

I threw a pillow at him, wincing as my head rewarded my efforts with a fresh throb of pain. I leaned it against the wall and closed my eyes. "Asshole."

"You said that."

"It's worth repeating."

He tossed the pillow back to me and it hit me in the chest, giving me a start. I wrapped my arms around it and hugged it against my chest.

"So, what happened? Did the old guy choke me out?" he asked. "The last thing I remember is his hands around my neck."

"Sort of. He tried to suck your magic out. But I put the kibosh on that. You passed out. He smacked me around a little and tried to suck magic out of me."

Dan smirked, looking toward the door. "How'd that work out for him?"

"He definitely got more than he bargained for."

"What does that mean?" He narrowed his eyes.

"C'mere. Give me your hand."

I received a wary look, but he scooted closer and placed his hand in mine. His fingers were warm and soft. The memory of John's work-roughened hands in mine rose unbidden. I shoved it away and closed my eyes. I tried to tap into my power, but it seemed like the binding the witch had placed on Dan was keeping me from drawing on his magic. I wasn't sure how to make it go the other way.

"Try to cast a spell," I said, opening my eyes to watch him.

"I can't, I'm—"

"Just try."

He tried, but nothing happened.

"Worth a shot. I thought maybe we could get around the binding."

He gave me a confused look, tightening his grip on my fingers when I tried to release his. "How?"

"When he used the spell on me, it didn't work because I'm not a witch. Or, at least not in the way you and the others are. I think he activated my ability, just... in reverse. The magic went through me into him, instead of through me into the ground."

Dan's brows shot up, and he put both of his hands in mine like that might help. "Try it again," he said, a note of pleading in his voice.

"I don't know how to reproduce it on demand. It just happened."

"Try it. I didn't know what you wanted before."

We tried for a while, but eventually, I pried my hands away and tucked them under my arms. "Sorry."

He was clearly disappointed, but waved the apology off and stood, walking over to a wooden chair that sat against the wall under one of the windows. Dan climbed up onto the chair and looked out the window.

"See anything?"

"Snow." He reached up to fiddle with the window. "I don't think it opens, and it's warded so I doubt we can smash it."

"Doesn't look big enough to climb out of anyway. Is there anything we can use for a weapon? Maybe we can get the drop on him when he comes back to... do whatever it is he intends to do with us."

Dan hopped down and started to search the room. He didn't get very far before the door opened forcefully.

"You," our captor said, his less-than-imposing frame not quite filling the doorway. He pointed at me. "Get up, and come with me."

"No way." Dan stepped between me and the older witch. "It's power you want, right? Take mine, and let her go."

His chivalrous display surprised me, to say the least. I couldn't help but wonder what his angle was, because Dan didn't have a self-sacrificing bone in his body. Or did he? If the last fifteen minutes had taught me anything, it was that I didn't know my baby brother as well as I'd thought.

The older man paused, fixing my brother with a calculating stare. The next thing I knew, a casual display of power sent Dan flying. He slammed into a chest of drawers with a clatter and thud and hit the ground on his hands and knees. It happened so fast, I'd barely even seen the spell. That was scary, I'll admit. Even during the duel upstairs earlier, the magic hadn't been flying quite that fast.

I sat up abruptly, holding up both hands. "Whoa there, take it easy. I'm coming." I scooted toward the edge of the bed, moving a little gingerly on account of the throbbing in my skull.

Dan wasn't down for the count. I could see him moving, pushing himself up, a split lip dripping blood down his chin. "Em, no..." he said, imploring me with his eyes to stay back.

"It's okay. It's not like he can burn me out, right? Can't take what I don't have." I settled my eyes on the witch in the doorway and kept them there, the wary glance of a weaker animal to an alpha. I hated myself for it. I wanted to be stronger. Surer. He didn't look angry, or even aggressive. Somehow, it made him seem even more dangerous. Unpredictable.

"Where are we going?" I asked, moving gingerly across the room.

"Not far." He stepped out of the doorway so I could exit the room. When I did, he closed the door firmly on Dan's continued protestations and locked it. The silence in the hall once the door shut was absolute. I couldn't even hear Dan pounding on the door, though it shook in its frame as he did.

"Do I even want to know why you have a guest room in your basement that only locks on the outside?" My snark was a front, a shield, a warm blanket to wrap around myself as if it could insulate me from chilly gusts of nervous anxiety.

He didn't answer, but a magical glow sprung to life around him. I flinched back, fetching up against the wall beside the door.

"What are you doing? What do you want from me?" Even as I spoke the words, I knew what he wanted. Power.

He'd been draining witches of it all over town. He'd tried to take my brother's, and then he found me. Chances were he didn't even know what I was or how my ability worked—hell, I barely understood it myself. But he'd found exactly what he wanted. Power. I just didn't know what he intended to do with it.

"I'm sorry." He grabbed my wrist. I tried to pull away, but his fingers were like a goddamn vise. "I hope this doesn't hurt too much."

"It's not too late. Just let us go, we won't tell any—" I didn't get any further, because he did that thing again. This time I saw the spell come together, lines of power twisting in the air a moment before they plunged into my chest.

I'm not sure how long I stood there while he sucked power through me, but by the time he was done, I knew what a narrow straw felt like when a thick milkshake was forced through it. I fell to my knees when he released me, unable to remain upright. He held something in his hand, something that dangled, swayed and crackled with lingering mystical energy. He'd been feeding the power he drew through me into it, somehow.

"What... is that?" I could barely speak the words. I was panting, sweating and shivering all at once. Like I'd just run a marathon in below-freezing weather or had mind-blowing sex. I think I would've preferred either, even the marathon, to what had actually happened.

Again, he didn't answer. Instead, he unlocked the door and dragged me by one arm to heave me back inside. I hit the floor with both knees and barely caught myself on shaking arms.

"Emily!" Dan rushed to my aid. "What'd you do to her, you sick fuck?"

"I'm sorry," the witch said. He even sounded sincere.

With my face buried in Dan's shoulder, I heard the door shut and the telltale click of the lock.

"Are you okay?" Dan rubbed my back and rocked me slowly. "Shit, what did he do?"

It took me a few moments to summon the strength to answer. "He had some kind of talisman. A necklace, I think. He drew a shit ton of power through me and fed it to it. I don't know why."

"A necklace?" I could practically hear his ears perking. "What kind of necklace? What did it look like?"

I groaned and shook my head slowly. "I dunno, I was too busy being a straw."

Dan eyed me with obvious concern for my mental health. "We've got to get out of here."

I couldn't have agreed more.

CHAPTER 32

The next time Mr. Magic-Sucker opened the door, we were ready for him. We'd positioned ourselves beside the door, as flat against the wall as possible. I held my breath for good measure. When the witch stepped into the seemingly empty room to look for his captives, carrying a tray with a plate of sandwiches and two bottles of water, Dan clocked him upside the head with the lamp from the bedside table. The pottery shattered on impact with our captor's skull, but it had the intended effect. The older man dropped like a sack of bricks.

"Wow, it actually worked." Dan tossed the remains of the lamp aside.

I rolled the man onto his side and checked for a pulse. It thrummed steady and strong under my fingers.

Dan grabbed my arm and towed me toward the door. "We need to get the hell out of here before he wakes up. Come on!"

I went with him, reassured that the witch was still alive. He may have been an unethical asshole, but I didn't want to do prison time as an accomplice. Granted, we would've had a good case for self-defense.

We made it up the basement stairs and spilled out into the kitchen without incident. We were halfway across the kitchen when a child's cry of distress reached my ears. I put on the brakes, but Dan kept going, dragging me by the hand.

"Dan! Wait!"

"It's a trap!"

"It could be, but what if he's got another captive?"

That stalled him. He eyed me uncertainly, then shook his head. "We get out, we call the cops. Let them be the heroes."

I let Dan pull me toward the door, but I'll be damned if that kid's cry didn't stick with me. My hand to god, I felt my ovaries clench. I was on the verge of insisting we search the house, but it turned out to be unnecessary. A mundie girl stood in the mouth of the hall outside. She couldn't have been more than six, and despite the fact that the sun was still up she wore a frilly pink nightgown and looked like she'd just rolled out of bed.

"Who are you?" the child asked, lifting a small fist to scrub at one eye. A teddy bear dangled from that fist, clutched tightly.

Dan stared at her as if he'd never seen a child before, leaving me to pick up the slack.

"I'm Emily, and this is Dan. What's your name?"

"Alice."

I offered her my most friendly nurse smile and bent down to her level. "Where's your mommy, Alice?"

Alice gazed at me with solemn blue eyes. "Mommy's with the angels." A smile blossomed on her face. "Are you the angel that's come to make me better?"

Puzzled, I looked her over with a clinical eye. Alice was a little on the skinny side, but she looked healthy. In my line of work, though, I knew appearances could be deceiving. "No, sweetie, I'm not an angel."

Dan leaned over and whispered, "Is that the talisman?"

It took me a moment to figure out what he was talking about, but there it was. Hanging around the little girl's neck on a golden chain, nestled in the satiny fabric covering her narrow chest, was the piece of jewelry that our captor had super-charged. I couldn't sense its power in the slightest; it could've been any random piece of jewelry.

I reached for it instinctively, wondering why the girl was wearing it.

Alice recoiled as if my fingers had sprouted claws, slapping her hand over the talisman. "Mine!" she growled, a sudden fierce glint in her eyes.

Blinking, I quickly withdrew my hand. "It's okay, Alice, I won't take it from you. I just wanted to look. It's very pretty."

Alice took another distrustful step back. Light began to peek out between her fingers, which curled around the amulet a moment later. Her fist began to glow, radiating magical energy. She screwed up her face and bellowed. "Daddy!"

Dan grabbed my arm. "Time to go."

I let him tow me toward the door, but kept my eyes glued on Alice. The magical energy spread down her arm and across her shoulders. Astonished, I tripped over my own feet and went sprawling. Pain radiated up the knee and arm I landed on, but I managed to jerk my head back and avoided making chin contact with the tile floor. Dan scrambled to help me up.

"Daddy!" Alice screamed at the top of her lungs. "What did you do to my daddy?"

My heart raced. I limped for the door, afraid to look back. I could sense the power behind me without looking. It sang to me, a beacon of warmth and light at my back. Curiosity got the better of me. While Dan threw open the locks, I looked back. Alice had followed us. Her entire small body radiated light. If I hadn't known better, I would've thought she was a witch. What was the amulet doing?

Alice dropped her bear and brought her hands up, touching a fingertip to a thumb and walking her hands up in the air as if she were singing the Itsy Bitsy Spider song. Dan tugged on my arm, but all I could do was stare as magic danced between Alice's fingertips. Her thin blond hair lifted at the sides as the air around her took on a static charge. It was so much power for one small body. Too much, I feared.

I shook off Dan's hand and took a step toward Alice. "Hey, Alice. Take a deep breath for me, okay? We're not here to hurt you or your daddy."

"Em, don't!" Dan called after me.

Alice drew her hands apart. The lines of her spell hovered in the air between them like fine spun gold. I had no idea what it was. All I knew was that I needed to calm her down before she harmed herself. Or us.

"Where's my daddy?" Alice asked, her eyes boring into mine.

"He's downstairs, uh, sleeping."

Alice didn't buy it. She narrowed her eyes, then brought her hands together with a tiny clap. As she did, the spell shrunk into a concentrated ball of energy and shot toward me. Dan shoved me aside. I hit the wall hard, rattling the picture frames, but Dan went flying backward as the magical bolt struck him dead center. He hit the wall beside the open door and slumped to the floor, inches from freedom but unconscious.

I lunged for Alice and caught her small wrists before she could do any more damage, hoping that she needed her hands for spell casting. That was how witches learned as children, with gestures, but as they got older they usually grew beyond needing them. Had the witch taught his daughter—a mundie who had no scrap of magic in her that I could detect—to use the magic stored in the amulet? I had no idea that was even possible.

Alice screamed and thrashed in my grasp, radiating magical energy at an alarming rate. I took a deep breath and opened myself to it, embracing my newfound gift. Heat slid into my hands and up my arms as the magic flooded my body. I let it come, let it slide through my torso, down my legs, and into the floor.

The glow around Alice dimmed, and the corresponding flow of magic coursing through me weakened. I siphoned the magic off until all that was left was a faint glow around the talisman. Alice's struggles had weakened by then, and I released one of her hands to grab the talisman, snapping the slender golden chain around the girl's throat and yanking the object of power away.

Alice went quiet, and her eyes turned vacant. Her knees buckled. She hung from my one-handed grip until I released her, then dropped to her knees and slumped forward. Confused, I caught her and eased her down onto the tile.

"Alice?" I patted her cheek, but she lay there staring up at nothing, completely unresponsive. I checked her pulse and watched the slow rise and fall of her chest. She was alive but catatonic. Tori's face flickered in my mind, the similarities in their conditions difficult to ignore. I looked from the amulet in my hand to Alice's pale, expressionless face and back again as the pieces finally started clicking into place.

"Get away from her!" Our captor's voice boomed as he thundered across the tile toward me, glowing with magical power.

I slapped the amulet against Alice's chest, knowing there was a little bit of juice left in it.

The child's lashes fluttered, and she stirred beneath my hand. "Daddy?"

His angry expression melted, and he dropped to his knees across from me. "I'm here, baby." He grabbed her discarded teddy bear and handed it to her.

Alice curled an arm around her bear and smiled, relaxed and happy but obviously tired. I lifted the amulet from her chest experimentally, watching as her face went slack and her eyes unfocused. Alice wasn't a mundie. She was a burned-out witch, and somehow the amulet with its stolen magic made her whole again.

The witch's hand lashed out, his fist closing around mine as they clutched the amulet. "Please." His eyes pleaded along with his words, and the energy around him dissipated like a white flag being waved.

I yanked my hand from his grasp. "How long has she been like this?"

He hung his head, shoulders slumped. "Six months."

I blinked. Even if Escobar's partner had been his first victim, which we had no evidence of, that had only been three weeks ago. Were there others that we didn't know about?

"When did you— How did you—" I couldn't decide what to ask first.

"Please give me the necklace."

I withdrew farther, tightening my grip on the amulet. "Not until you tell me what's going on. Tell me everything."

He sighed and stroked Alice's baby-fine hair. "We were on our way home from one of Alice's soccer games. I don't remember the accident itself. They told me a drunk driver ran a stop sign and hit the driver's side head-on. My wife was driving." He glanced at the wall of family portraits with grief-stricken eyes. "They said she died on impact. I got away with cracked ribs and a few scrapes, but I lost consciousness. When I came to, the first thing I became aware of was magic, powerful magic, seemingly all around me. It was Alice. She was trying to heal her mother."

I stared at him for a moment, slack-jawed. "You taught her healing magic? At her age?" Healing magic was powerful shit, well beyond many seasoned practitioners. To even attempt to teach it to a child? It boggled my mind.

He winced, but continued, "I knew she was a bit young, but I've always had a knack for it. I thought it'd be okay to teach her a few simple spells. Healing minor scratches, that sort of thing. She started bringing home stray animals, and we'd patch them up together before taking them to the shelter. What I didn't count on was how damn smart she is. How observant."

"You performed more complicated spells in front of her."

"Yes. And she tried to use them on Lindsey, who was probably too far gone even for me. Alice... she wouldn't quit. She just kept pouring more and more magic into the spell. I called out to her, tried to stop her, but I could barely breathe and couldn't get the seat belt unbuckled. She burned out before my eyes."

Anger and pity bubbled inside me. This idiotic man had

given his child the metaphysical equivalent of a loaded handgun and was then shocked and dismayed when she pulled the trigger. But the thought of poor distraught Alice, kneeling beside her mother's broken, lifeless body, trying to will her back to life... the mental image sent a shiver down my spine. I uncurled my fingers and looked down at the amulet. Its lingering magic sang to me.

I held it up. "Where did you get this?"

"It's a family heirloom. I'd all but forgotten about it until after the accident. All I knew about it was that it stored magic. I'd never needed it."

The arrogance in his words brought a knowing smile to my lips. Those sorts of objects were considered crutches for weaker witches. "So, you got the idea to feed it some magic and put it on her?"

He nodded. "You've seen it in action. I got my little girl back."

The pieces still didn't quite connect. I turned the amulet over in my fingers, thinking. "So, what went wrong?"

"I started using my own magic at first, but after a few months, it wasn't enough. She needed more and more, so I looked for... alternative sources."

"Draining other witches dry, you mean."

He grimaced. "I'm still fine-tuning the spell."

"So, you what... started slipping witches you thought no one would miss spelled coins to use as focus objects for remote magic sucking?"

His eyes widened, but he didn't deny it. "Who— Who are you?" He shook his head, not waiting for an answer. "I never meant to hurt anyone, I swear. You can't imagine what it's like, to lose her like that, over and over. I had to do what I did. But now that you're here, I don't have to anymore."

I blinked, visions of being locked in his basement for the rest of Alice's long life flashing through my mind.

Oh. Hell. No.

I rocked to my feet. "No. Absolutely not. We're leaving." I knew he had the means to overpower me again, easily, but I've never been short on stubbornness.

"No, wait! You don't understand."

"I understand perfectly, and I'm not going to be your personal magic battery. You can't hold us here forever."

"I don't need to. With your help, I think— No, I know. I can heal her."

I stared at him. The suggestion was preposterous. Ludicrous. Witches didn't come back from burnout. They couldn't be healed. Everyone knew that, even a null like me. "Do you think I was born yesterday? Gimme a break."

His eyes pleaded with me. "No, please. It's like I said. I have a gift for healing. I just don't have the kind of power it would take to do it on my own. But with your help, I know can pull it off."

There was an earnestness to him that told me he did believe it, even if it was delusional. I glanced over my shoulder at Dan. He was still out cold, which was a pity. I would've liked to hear what he had to say about all this. I just wanted to go home, to wash my hands of all this and bury my head back in the sand. But when I looked down at the little girl in the frilly pink nightie, I'll be damned if the sight of her didn't tug at my heartstrings. Either way, I met the witch's eyes again and gave him my best no-nonsense look.

"I'll help you, on one condition."

He clasped his hands in front of him, a picture of desperation. "Anything you want. If it's in my power, I promise I'll do it."

"You get one shot. Whether it succeeds or fails, my brother and I get to walk away. From this moment on, we're not your prisoners."

"Done," he said quickly—a little too quickly for my taste, but beggars can't be choosers.

CHAPTER 33

We moved Alice to the kitchen table and got Dan settled on the couch. It bugged me that he was still out cold, but his pupils were reactive when I checked. Plus, hard-headedness was kind of a family trait, so I wasn't too worried.

The witch tucked Alice's teddy bear under her arm and stood opposite me at the table with Alice between us. He held his hands out, palms up. The amulet sat atop one of them. I placed my hand in the other. The glow of magic sprang to life around him, and I watched as the threads of the spell came together, bracing myself for the onslaught.

Dread squeezed my stomach. My mouth went dry.

"Wait," I blurted as the spell loomed closer.

He paused, giving me an inquisitive look.

"What's your name?"

"My name?"

I nodded.

"Charles. Charles Adams."

"Okay, Chuck. Let me try something, before you..." I motioned at the spell hovering in the air. He released the threads that held it together, and it wisped away to nothing. I wanted to close my eyes, but I didn't trust him enough. Instead, I let them unfocus and expanded my senses, searching for the tingle of energy I knew resided under my hand. I'd only ever successfully tapped into my ability out of desperation at that point, but it was more familiar to me now that I'd done it a few times intentionally. I drew a deep breath and imagined myself pulling Charles's magic in with it. My fingers tingled as the first hint of power flowed between us. I sucked in another breath, and the magic flowed more freely.

"What are you doing?" Charles said, pulling his hand away. Or trying.

I tightened my grip. "Give me a minute."

His power filled me, flowing from my fingers through my body, down my legs and into the floor at my feet. I expanded my awareness of it, feeling it connect with the magic in the earth. Charles pulled harder at my hand, but I didn't let go. It was time to find out what I could really do. Kassidy had told me that my ability might work both ways. I knew now that it did. I just didn't know if I could initiate it consciously.

I took another deep breath, then exhaled slowly. Deliberately. I focused on the flow of energy, remembering what it felt like for Charles to pull the magic through me, and willed the stream of magic to reverse its course. It took a few seconds, but it worked. When I let my eyes focus again, I found Charles staring at me wide-eyed, the glow around him brighter than before. Willing myself not to smirk, I motioned with my free hand for him to get on with it.

He cleared his throat and set to work, weaving lines of power into an intricate tapestry while I stood watching, magic flowing freely between us. It was like standing in a cool stream, the magic washing through me like crisp spring water. As the minutes drew on, and the spell gained complexity, sweat beaded on Charles's forehead.

"More," he said, licking his lips as if parched.

I hesitated, unsure if I could give him more—and of what would happen if I tried. His eyes met mine over the table, and he repeated his request. Nibbling the inside of my lip, I closed my eyes and imagined myself as a pipe the magic flowed through, focused on expanding it into a wider channel so that more could slip through. Nothing happened, so I shifted my focus to the magic itself, willing it to flow faster. With a surge, it did, like a flash flood through a creek bed. The sensation was less pleasant than the gently flowing stream, but still preferable to being on the receiving end of Charles's spell. The floodgate was open, but it hadn't been battered down.

After a few moments, I registered the death grip Charles had on my hand. When I opened my eyes, he stood hunched over and gasping, as if it were too much. I dialed it back instinctively, but his fingers clamped down even harder.

"Leave it," he said. "It's fine. It's good."

"Are you sure?"

He gave me a tight nod, and I let him have it. Shuddering, he closed his eyes and a few seconds later, his grip on my hand eased. He opened his eyes and straightened, going back to work on his spell which hovered in the air over Alice. There was so much magic coursing through him that the whites of his eyes glowed, the way that witch's had in the ER last week. If I hadn't already known he was pushing his limits, that would've cinched it.

By then, the spell matrix was nearly as wide as Alice was tall, a complex three-dimensional construct that actually hurt my head when I tried to focus on it too hard. I'd never seen anything like it. Granted, I hadn't spent a lot of time watching witches cast intricate spells. I had twenty-eight years of self-preservative apathy built up. Wanting to be able to use magic had never gotten me anywhere, never caused me anything but heartache. Yes, there was a time when I wanted to be a "real witch" more than anything, but wanting it couldn't make it happen. I'd left that desire long ago, or at least convinced myself that I had.

But now that I knew what it felt like to feel magic coursing through me, I wondered what else I could do. Was there more to being a Conduit than I'd discovered? Could I learn to cast spells while I was connected to a witch this way? For that matter, could I learn to pull magic into me without being connected to a witch? And if I could, would I be able to do anything with it?

I had so many questions, but it wasn't the time to explore them. I looked away from the increasingly complicated spell. My eyes settled on Alice, and I watched her narrow chest rise and fall slowly as she slept, her pale blond hair tousled around her small head. The idea that Charles might be able to restore her was far-fetched, but I wouldn't have felt right if I didn't let him try. Sure, he was basically a metaphysical rapist who'd been violating witches in the worst way, leaving behind broken husks that lacked the will to go on living. But Alice— Alice was an innocent. For a child to lose her magic so young? My heart ached for her. If there was a snowball's chance in Phoenix that she could be healed, it was worth it.

The seconds ticked by, turning into minutes. I checked in on Charles again. His features were drawn in intense focus, and his face had a haggard quality to it. Sweat ran down his face in rivulets, and he had damp patches under his arms. His grip on my fingers was firm, but his hand had begun to tremble.

I opened my mouth to ask if he was okay, but hesitated to distract him. Before I could make up my mind which way to go, the spell hovering over Alice sank, disappearing into her. My eyes widened in alarm, but Charles's face showed no hint that this was unexpected. He reached out and lay his free hand on her chest, and I continued watching as the golden glow around him spread out beneath his fingertips, licking across his daughter's torso.

"More," he said, voice hoarse.

Studying him, I frowned. "I don't think that's a good idea."

He looked up, meeting my eyes. "Please, Emily. I'm so close."

"I don't think you can take much more. You won't be any help to her if you burn yourself out."

"I can take it. I can do this. I have to do this. Please."

I glanced down at Alice again, worrying my lower lip between my teeth. Then I folded both my hands around his and cranked it up to eleven. His back arched and he cried out sharply, but the glow spreading from his fingers quickly grew to cover Alice's entire body, until they were both lit up like the Fourth of July. Alice sucked in a deep breath all of a sudden, and her eyes popped open. Charles's hand remained firm on her chest as she looked up at him, confusion plain upon her small features.

Charles screamed, his mouth twisted in a painful grimace. His body went rigid and convulsed as the connection between us snapped. Power rushed back at me with enough force that I stumbled backwards. I hit the wall behind me, my vision swimming as I struggled against the backlash to remain upright.

But the magic bled slowly back out, flowing down my trembling body and into the ground once more. I put a hand to my throbbing head and peeled my tongue off the roof of my suddenly dry mouth. When the room stopped spinning, I saw Alice sitting up on the table, clutching her teddy bear and staring at me with big blue eyes. The glow that'd been around her had vanished, but I could still sense the magic inside her. He'd done it. She was intact.

Charles, however, was nowhere to be seen.

I rushed around the table and found him on the floor. "Charles!"

Kneeling beside him, I felt for his pulse and found it, thready but present. His chest rose and fell slowly, but his eyes... His eyes were open, glassy, staring at nothing. There wasn't even a hint of magic left in him. My throat constricted and my eyes stung. I told myself that he wasn't worth crying over, that he'd burned out at least three witches in a desperate, selfish bid to buy more time with his daughter. But I'd known what the consequence could be when I gave him that last boost of power, and I'd done it anyway. His condition was as much my fault as it was his.

"Daddy!" Alice cried, looking over the edge of the table.

I hastily swiped a tear from my cheek. "He's okay, sweetie. He's just sleeping."

Alice scrambled down off the table to join us on the floor. "His eyes are open."

"Sometimes daddies do that," I said around the knot in my throat. "So they can watch out for their little girls even when they're asleep."

She accepted this explanation with the innocence of youth and tucked her teddy bear under his arm before looking at me again. "Can I go play, now?"

"Uh, sure. But stay in the house, okay?"

"Okay!" She hopped to her feet and ran off.

I watched in awe, scarcely able to believe this exuberant child was the same one that'd been so still, practically lifeless, mere moments ago. Shaking my head, I sat back on my heels and noticed the glint of a gold chain sticking out of Charles's pocket. The amulet. I plucked it free and tucked it in my own pocket for safekeeping, then went looking for a phone so I could call the police.

CHAPTER 34

I'm not going to pretend that Escobar didn't give me an earful when we got back to the station, or that Andy and Michelle didn't give me a hard time about being on the wrong end of a callout for the second time that week. But after the day I'd had, I welcomed the harassment since it came—in both cases—with the opportunity to let the professionals take over.

Dan and I stopped at the Tin Whistle to pick up dinner on the way home, and within an hour of fleeing the police station with my dignity mostly intact, I was kicking back on my sofa with a steak burrito the size of my face, admiring the new painting propped up against the entertainment center. That's right. I bought that landscape I'd been admiring, figuring I deserved to treat myself after a long week of family drama and crime-fighting.

You'll never guess whose name was on the artist card: John Warren.

What were the odds that it'd turn out to be the same tall, dark, and sexy firefighter that'd run to the rescue and helped me get answers about my fledgling abilities? I had no idea. But I still felt good about my purchase. The walls in my apartment had been barren for far too long, and something about the painting had called to me.

I was two bites into my burrito when a loud knock interrupted my meal. I glanced at my brother. "Wanna get that?"

"Your house," he said around a bite of his enchilada.

"You live here too, now. And you're not paying rent, so answer the damn door."

"Alright, alright, I'm going." He dropped his styrofoam to-go container on the coffee table and headed for the door. I noticed Barrington eyeing the unattended food from the foot of the couch. His pupils expanded until there was barely a hint of iris around them.

I leaned over and folded the lid closed. "Don't even think about it, you little glutton."

Dan unlocked the door and opened it, then slammed it shut immediately and threw his back against it like he expected it to explode inward. I sat up, frowning.

"What's wrong?"

Dan didn't get a chance to reply, because the door did fly open with a burst of magic that sent him staggering away. A tall Native American man with sharp cheekbones and long dark hair stepped into the doorway, surrounded by a glowing magical nimbus. The air around him all but crackled with energy, and his dark eyes glinted with anger.

I was on my feet in a flash, my food abandoned beside Dan's. "Hey! You can't just bust in here. That's called breaking and entering."

He ignored me and strode forward, grabbed Dan by the throat, and slammed him against the wall beside the door. "Where's my money?"

Magic flickered around Dan as he tried to summon the power to defend himself, but something about how the guy was cutting off his air must've made it difficult. He clawed at his assailant's hand, trying to pry his fingers loose the old-fashioned way. I made a mental note as I strode across the room. Maybe in the future, I shouldn't spend so much time fighting the urge to throttle Dan.

While my brother struggled for breath, rendered unable to answer the question by the very man who'd asked it, I headed for the envelope of cash on the dining table. It never had been entered into evidence, since we weren't sure if it was connected to the attacks. I swiped the envelope and walked it over to the men—and I use the term loosely.

"Hey." I smacked his shoulder and held up the envelope. "Joseph, right? You looking for this?"

He nodded and made a grab for the envelope, but I danced out of his reach. "Let my brother go, and you can have it."

Joseph's eyes narrowed, but he released Dan, who wheezed in a gasping breath and bent over, hands on knees.

"You alright?" I asked, my eyes on Dan as I handed Joseph the envelope.

Dan waved a hand and kept sucking in air like it was candy on Christmas.

"Where's the rest?" Joseph asked, glancing at Dan. At least he'd released the magic he was holding, so I didn't feel like I needed sunglasses to look at him.

I thumped Joseph on the shoulder, I guess because poking bears was my specialty. "He didn't have it, you belligerent asshole." I waited for him to turn his attention to me before I went on. "I got it from a burned-out kid on the Pueblo."

I expected him to ask me which one, but he surprised me. "Luke?"

"Yeah, you know him?"

He nodded, deep lines edged in his forehead as he tucked the money away. "His sister babysits for us. He's the one that found Christina, after..." He shook his head. "I heard about his accident. But how did he get this?"

Naturally, Dan took that moment to find his gravelly voice. "Ask your wife."

Joseph's jaw tightened. He turned back toward Dan with menace in his eyes, but I grabbed his arm before he could close the distance. If he'd really wanted to hit my brother, I doubt I could've stopped him. The guy was seriously built.

"Okay, that's enough! Both of you." I stepped between them, facing Joseph. "Did you cash your check at Del Norte Credit Union?"

He nodded.

"There was a witch there, giving out spelled coins. He used them as focuses to steal magic from a distance. That's what happened to Christina and Luke. Luke must've taken the money when he found Christina. It ended up with one of his relatives, and—long story short—he gave it to me. Dan had nothing to do with it."

Joseph looked past me at Dan, hands curling into fists at his sides. Not exactly the reaction I'd been going for, to be honest. He batted me aside and reached for my brother, but it was an open hand he offered instead of a fist. "I'm sorry, Dan. I misjudged you."

Dan eyed the outstretched hand as if it held some hidden agenda, but reached out and shook it after a moment. "It happens."

Joseph didn't linger long after that. Once the door was shut behind him and propped shut with a chair from the dining table—I was going to have to put in a maintenance request to get the doorjamb fixed—I hastened to rescue my dinner from the cat. But fortunately, the commotion seemed to have sent him into hiding.

"How's it feel to have your reputation restored?" I asked, kicking my feet up on the coffee table as Dan joined me on the couch once more.

He shrugged. "It wasn't that great to start with."

"We can work on that…"

Dan poked at his food, his features taking on a pensive cast. "I'd like that."

Just when I think I've got him figured out, he goes and surprises me again.

CHAPTER 35

I kept an eye on Charles while he was at St. Vincent's. His condition didn't improve—not that I expected it to —but he remained stable. Alice went into foster care, but it only took a few days for social services to locate her maternal grandparents. I crossed paths with them at the hospital once when they brought Alice to visit Charles. The next day, Charles was moved to hospice and off my radar.

Things pretty much went back to normal after that. You'd think it would've been a relief, that after the most eventful week of my life to date, settling back into my normal routine would've been just what I needed. Instead, it was quite the opposite. I was restless. Unsettled. I even went out on a third date with Barry, despite Dan's relentless teasing about watching for hairballs and inappropriate public grooming rituals.

Seriously, he didn't shut up until I threatened to call Hector the next time he went out for drinks with the coven leader's girlfriend. Dan may have gotten his groove back, magically speaking, but even though he insisted there was nothing going on between him and Tracy, he wasn't eager for a confrontation with Hector.

It took me a while, and a few pointed remarks from Matt, to figure out what was bothering me. In the wake of all the excitement, the day-to-day drudgery of life was driving me nuts. As dangerous as my foray into crime-fighting had been, as freaked out as I had been—and still was—about my awakening powers, it had made me feel special in a way I never had before... like I had something to offer the world besides my bedside manner and an endless wellspring of useless trivia.

Maybe that's why my heartbeat kicked up a notch when I walked out of the hospital at the end of a particularly tedious night shift a few weeks later to find one Detective Michael Escobar leaning against the fender of my car. His eyes were on his phone, so I took advantage of his distraction to get my reaction under control and give him a moment's perusal. He looked the same as he always had. Maybe a little better rested. By the time he looked up and saw me, I had my expression mostly under control.

"Hey there, detective. I hope you're not here to arrest me."

He smirked and tucked his phone in his back pocket. "Not today."

Gulp.

I laughed nervously and shook my head. "Well, that's good. What can I do ya for?"

"Got a case I could use some help on. Rash of break-ins, magical stuff going missing. What's your brother got going on these days?"

"Oh. Uh, being annoying and looking for work, mostly." My disappointment was palpable, and I struggled to keep it from my face. "You want me to give him a—"

He held up a hand, laughing. "Just messing with you. You should see your face. Actually, I was hoping you might let me buy you a cup of coffee."

I blinked slowly. "Like... a date?" That definitely wasn't what I'd been expecting.

"Oh, god no!" He winced. "I mean, not that you're not— I'm not— Shit, that came out wrong."

I laughed. "No offense taken."

He rubbed a hand down his face. "This is off to a great start. We're still having trouble finding a full-time consultant for Magic Crimes. I was wondering if you might be interested in some more work, on an ongoing basis."

"Oh? Hmm." I leaned against the car beside him, feigning reluctance. "I dunno, I'm pretty busy. And it didn't pay much."

"I know. And I can't offer you more, not right off the bat. But once you show the chief how much of an asset you can be..."

I thought about the application he'd given me, the one that was still tucked behind my sun visor. "Do I have to register?"

He gave me the side-eye. "You trying to make me change my mind about arresting you?"

"I'm not a witch."

God. I sounded petulant even to myself.

"Your parents are witches, right? Your brother?"

"You know they are." I grimaced, regretting bringing it up. I should've known he wouldn't let me consult unless my application was stamped, sealed, and notarized. But the idea of putting my name in that database left a sour feeling in my stomach. It was publicly searchable, for one, and there were plenty of people out there that reviewed it like it was a sexual predator registry, keeping an eye on what kind of element was moving into their neighborhood. But more than that, it was a public acknowledgment of something I still hadn't fully come to terms with myself: I wasn't a null.

I might not be able to use magic, but it sure as hell could use me. I sighed and tipped my head back, looking up at the gray sky. The air was bitter cold and smelled like fresh snow was coming. "What I don't think you get is what you're asking me to do."

"Obey the law. That's what I'm asking you to do. What did you expect? I'm a cop. The law is kind of my thing."

"Could we circle back to that date thing? That's sounding more appealing by the second."

He snorted and pushed off the fender. "You had your chance, Davenport. Once you turn down all of this"—he gestured at himself—"you don't get a second chance."

"It's Emily."

"What?"

"My name. It's Emily."

He eyed me like I was an escaped mental patient. "Right..."

I summoned a wan smile. "I mean, you should probably call me by my first name if we're going to be working together."

"Only if you call me Mike." Grinning, he stuck out his hand.

I shook it, sealing the deal. "When do I start?"

"No time like the present. I really do have a case I could use some help on." He pulled a consultant badge from his pocket and dropped it into my hand. The plain white lanyard had been replaced with a dark green one with black cats and witches riding broomsticks on it. "Come on, you can ride to the station with me. I'll drop you off back here later."

I eyed him as I slipped the lanyard over my neck, then covered a jaw-cracking yawn with one hand. I'd been up all night, after all. "Can we stop for coffee and donuts on the way?"

He laughed. "This is the start of a beautiful partnership."

∽

AUTHOR'S NOTE

I started Emily's story about a year before I wrote the first Grant Wolves book, and I've been wanting to get back to it ever since.

I'm glad I did, and I hope you are too!

I seem to have a penchant for stories about women who are estranged from their mothers. I'd just like to state, for the record, that my mother is a wonderful person and we're very close (hi, Mom!).

Emily's crime-solving adventures will continue in 2020. In the meantime, I invite you to sign up for my newsletter (loridrakeauthor.com/subscribe) for release dates, sneak peeks, bonus content, free reads and more.

ABOUT THE AUTHOR

Disenchanted with her mundane human existence, Lori loves spinning tales of magic and creatures of myth & legend existing in the modern world. When not indulging in these flights of fancy, she enjoys cooking, crafting, gaming, and (of course) reading. She's also a bit of a weather geek and would like to go storm chasing one day.

Lori lives in Austin, Texas with her husband and three adorable kitties that don't understand why mommy doesn't like them climbing on her laptop and batting at the screen.

The kitties, that is. It'd be really strange if her husband did that.

www.loridrakeauthor.com
lori@loridrakeauthor.com

facebook.com/loridrakeauthor
bookbub.com/authors/lori-drake

Printed in Great Britain
by Amazon